Dr. Sheldon Kornpett opened the door to his private office and gestured for Vince to enter.

"The inner sanctum, huh?" Vince asked and going through the door said, "Remember that show on the radio, Inner Sanctum?"

What is it with this guy, Sheldon wondered? And how do I get rid of him?

"Could I borrow you for a couple of minutes?" asked Vince. "It's such a minor thing . . . " Vince looked almost embarrassed at having brought it up. "I'm almost embarrassed to ask but I just need a hand for maybe five minutes tops."

What the hell? Sheldon thought. Why not?

Vince rose, beaming. "Oh, Shel, this is just stupendously nice of you. And you might even enjoy it."

"Where are we going?"

"Just over to my office," Vince said. "I want you to break into my safe."

WARNER BROS. PRESENTS

"The In-Laws"

Starring

Peter Falk   Alan Arkin

Also Starring

NANCY DUSSAULT

FRAN DRESCHER

ARLENE GOLONKA

MICHAEL LEMBECK

RICHARD LIBERTINI

ED BEGLEY, JR.

Executive Producer ALAN ARKIN

Produced by WILLIAM SACKHEIM and
ARTHUR HILLER

Directed by ARTHUR HILLER

Original Screenplay by ANDREW BERGMAN

The In-Laws

a novel by
David Rogers

Based on an original
screenplay by Andrew Bergman

FAWCETT GOLD MEDAL • NEW YORK

THE IN-LAWS

© 1979 Warner Bros. Inc.

Published by Fawcett Gold Medal Books, a unit of CBS Publications, the Consumer Publishing Division of CBS Inc.

ISBN 0-449-14252-3

Printed in the United States of America

10 9 8 7 6 5 4 3 2 1

1

"Please."

"No."

"Why not?"

"I don't think we should."

"You don't want to."

"I do. You know how much I do."

"Then, why not?"

"Because I don't think we should."

The young man sighed forcefully, as much to let the girl know his frustration and annoyance as to expel the air. He removed his arms from around her, turned in the front seat of his father's Coupe de Ville, adjusted his underwear, and stared through the windshield at the dark suburban street in Teaneck, New Jersey. He had taken the Coupe de Ville instead of his own Volkswagen because his father was out of town anyway and he thought it would be more comfortable.

"Tommy," the girl whispered. She meant the two syllables to convey more than his name. Don't be angry, understand my feelings, and I love you, was what she had in mind. What Tommy heard behind the whispered name was, Persuade me.

He shifted back, embracing her again, breathing "Barbara" softly just before he kissed her. He meant the word to tell her, I understand your need to pretend that you think it's wrong and I'll go along with you as long as you intend to give in in a half-hour or so anyway. What Barbara heard was, I'm not angry. I'll wait. I love you.

It was a long kiss underscored by thoughts of soon and certain gratification on his part; certain gratification delayed by several days, the ceremony, the hors d'oeuvres, drinks, and the buffet lunch on hers.

At last Tommy pulled his lips from Barbara's and, nuzzling her cheek with his mouth, whispered, "Please," again.

"No," she replied.

"Why not?" he asked, and when they had gone over the entire text of the conversation once more, he removed his arms and turned away again, placing his hands on the steering wheel.

After a pause to pout, he spoke. "It's not as if we haven't done it already."

"That was before we were engaged," she said.

"I don't understand your reasoning."

"Well," she said, knowing her position was slightly ridiculous but feeling he should make some effort to understand, "the wedding is Sunday."

"But this is Wednesday night," he countered with an urgency that rose in pain from deep inside him.

"But if we wait, it'll be so much more wonderful on Sunday."

"It'll be just as wonderful now. *And* then."

"But we'd be on our honeymoon . . . at the Plaza," she added, suggesting the delights of a first-class hotel along with the honorable satisfaction of licit sex. When still he did not speak, she went on. "Besides, we can't go to your house and we can't go to mine and I hate that tacky motel scene." He was silent and she justified herself, telling herself it would all seem fresher, newer, more romantic when she was his wife. And even thinking the phrase "his wife" prompted her to add a wifely consideration to her argument. "Besides, Sunday is so soon and the motel would be a waste of money."

"I don't care about the money," he snapped.

Barbara felt a sudden jolt of fear. Was Tommy extravagant? Her father was a dentist, and, though he earned a good living, she had always been brought up to respect money, to save for a rainy day. Would she, in later years, in the event of a deluge, be caught with a profligate husband and no umbrella?

Why should she think about money at a time like this, Tommy wondered. Is she stingy? Will there be arguments about finance? Considering the cost of food, would she serve meatloaf every night?

They both sat silent, realizing in a flash that no matter how much one might love a spouse, marriage could present problems.

7

"Then you want me to take you home?" he asked into the dark, unmoving car.

"Well, no. Not really," she answered, hearing a hurt dismissal in his tone.

"We've had dinner," he reminded her.

"I guess so," she replied, defeated, and he put the car in gear.

It moved away from the curb quietly and down the dark, tree-lined street, where leaves glowed a startling green in pools of light from the street lamps.

"Your father . . ." Barbara began.

"Yes?" Tommy answered.

"He's all right for dinner tomorrow?"

"He knows about it. He'll be back in time," Tommy said with an assurance he did not quite feel. His father was away on another of his trips and while his intentions were always good, Tommy thought, his sense of time or the pressures of his mysterious work occasionally upset the best-made plans.

"My folks are anxious to meet him," Barbara said. "I mean . . . it's been a long time . . . and the wedding is Sunday. They feel a little funny about . . ." She let the sentence dwindle out.

"He's been real hung up," Tommy answered. "It's like . . . well, it's like his busy season. He wants to meet them, too."

"Yeah," she agreed, knowing they both understood the premarital tensions of their parents.

He turned the car into Barbara's street, realizing that after Sunday it would be Barbara's parents' street, his in-laws' street, and hers would be another one. His, too. He drove into the driveway of Barbara's house.

Barbara leaned over and kissed him. "I can't wait for Sunday," she said.

"Yes, you can," he said a little more sharply than he wished.

"Well, you know what I mean," she said.

"Yes," he replied softly, apologizing his way. "Me too." He kissed her more ardently then, releasing her only when he saw a sliver of light appear from behind an upstairs window in her . . . in her father's house.

"Tomorrow night," she said, sliding out of the car.

"Seven," he answered, and they both puckered, kissing the air between them. Barbara slammed the door and hurried up to the house. He watched until she was inside then drove off thinking, Tomorrow at seven . . . Sunday . . . and (with a strange but not unpleasant glow in the pit of his stomach) the rest of my life.

2

Thursday was gray, sunless, and sweaty in the capital city of the greatest country in the Western World. A large percentage of the citizens were going about the business of what was, in effect, a company town. The justices of the Supreme Court Court were hearing a case of such earth-shattering importance that none but ten lawyers out of two hundred million citizens could possibly understand or profit from it. On the Hill, members of the Congress were nit-picking their way through the creation of laws, complicated, vital, and resembling others they had passed the week before that the President, even now, was vetoing. Stenographers at various government departments were typing, Xeroxing, and allowing their bosses a quick grope in the supply room. At the Pentagon, staff sergeants made coffee by the numbers for colonels, as minor CIA officials worked on manuscripts of books they would publish as soon as they were fired.

In a less elegant section of the city, an area of warehouses, both occupied and abandoned, decaying rooming houses, and railroad yards, two uniformed men also advanced the business of their government. They advanced slowly, driving the armored car labeled *Department of the Treasury, U.S. Mint,* at roughly fifteen miles an hour over a bumpy, cobbled street. In the locked cab the driver hummed tunelessly against the melody of a Country-and-Western song that blasted from the radio.

"Let's call in, huh?" the guard beside him suggested, not nervously, just playing the game by the rules, thoughts of his pension always uppermost in his mind.

The driver nodded and, wordlessly, turned down the radio. The guard picked up the hand mike and pushed the button of the CB. "Hello," he called into the instrument. "This is Alpha and Beta. Over?" Actually, their names were Fred and Harold, but if you're playing the game, you play the game, he figured.

"We read you, Alpha . . . Beta. . . . Location?" a disembodied voice crackled back at them.

"We're whipping along South Factory," the guard answered. He checked his watch. "Should be coming into the old mint-o-roonie in about nine minutes at eleven hundred. Over."

"We're waitin' for ya, fellas," the static answered. Then it crackled, "Ten-four," and evaporated back into the atmosphere.

The driver swung the car one-handed through the wind-

12

ing narrow street, the other hand turning the volume up on the Country-and-Western music. He signalled a left turn, though there were no cars behind him, and drove along between a railroad yard on his left and a fenced construction site on his right. At the end of this new street he saw a huge construction crane obscuring the blinking yellow light of a train crossing behind it.

"Work train," the guard warned him.

"I see it," the driver answered and, sighing with annoyance—it was almost lunch time—braked before the barricade.

The two men sat staring at the train inching along in front of them, thinking their private thoughts, all sound blocked out by the blaring radio. They did not notice the construction crane swing around. It was only when they felt the jolt of the huge straps positioned firmly around the truck and almost simultaneously saw the ground sink from underneath them that terror descended on them.

"What the hell's goin' on?" the driver yelled, staring wide-eyed as his car went straight up like a helicopter.

The guard, who pride himself on his cool in a crisis, grabbed the CB microphone, pushed the button and shouted, "Base! This is Alpha-Beta. Come in . . . Come in, Base!"

He was still pushing the button and calling in frantically on the obviously jammed CB as the truck reached the height of the construction fence and, lurching to the right, swung over it and started down. As the armored car descended, they watched through the windshield as helmeted, goggled, ski-masked men, two of them carrying acetylene torches, came rushing toward the helpless vehicle.

"Fercrissakes . . ." the driver screamed, as the guard, valiantly continuing his hopeless task, howled into the microphone, "Keep trying, Base. Base . . . emergency! Come in, please. Come in."

The truck made a perfect four-point landing inside the construction site, although its passengers were too frightened to notice or think to compliment the construction-crane driver-pilot. As they touched the ground, the two men with the torches fired up, timing it perfectly, and, in unison, welded the doors shut on either side of the cab.

The two Treasury Department employees, by now in less than mint condition, banged frantically and fruitlessly against the shatterproof glass of the cab, not seeing or appreciating the well-timed choreography of two other masked workmen, who, with powerful drills, began to punch two holes through the back door of the armored car. Meanwhile a masked and goggled workman-conductor continued to orchestrate the snatch with a baton. Barking commands the two inside were unable to hear, he ordered other masked workmen to prepare a power winch twenty feet from the truck. Large claws were inserted into the holes in the rear door of the armored car and then attached to cables running from the power winch. Pointing dramatically, as to the brass section at the climax, the workman-conductor signaled the winch operator and, exploding with power, the cables snapped taut and the back of the armored car began to peel off.

Understanding completely now, the driver looked at his companion. "You can kiss them promotions goodbye," he said. The guard nodded sadly and they felt a joggle as the two masked workmen nearest them jumped into the back of the car.

14

Moving quickly in the confined space, the workmen shoved the first few bags and boxes of money out of the car, spilling fluttering bills, making a financial mess of the construction site. They moved amid the money, turning it over, searching under it, surprisingly uninterested in the cash, treating it like piles of old newspapers and magazines in some armored basement that concealed . . . what? It was an unlikely hunt through accessible treasure for buried treasure.

At last, kicking away a sack against the far wall of the truck, the face of one of the workmen lighted up beneath his ski mask. He poked his cohort and indicated a battered black bag beneath a stack of thousand-dollar bills. The cohort leaped forward, brushing away the bills as though they were dead leaves obscuring a flower bed. He snatched up the bag, released the catch, and opened it. Bringing it up to his chest, he dug his hand in, quickly checking the contents, then held it out to the other masked figure for his approval. The two men stared at the contents. Engravings, lots of engravings, the plates to print bills in the denominations of fifty, one hundred, and five hundred.

As his companion whistled soft, low, and appreciatively, the man snapped the bag shut and said, "That's the ticket. Let's go." He leaped out of the back of the truck, walking briskly but calmly away from the other man, who joined the rest of the masked crew.

Purposefully, the man with the bag walked on, turning a corner and stopping before an old, dilapidated warehouse. Peeling and sagging, the old building looked as thought it had once been busy and productive but now served only for assignations of romance or crime while it waited for its Social Security checks.

The man with the bag pushed open the creaking door and walked through an entranceway. A dim, bare bulb hung from the ceiling. He crossed a large, deserted floor, his footsteps echoing off the dust. He entered an ancient freight elevator and, operating the mechanism, started its heaving, rattling ascent to the top floor. When the elevator wheezed to a stop, he hurried down a dark corridor to a door. Passing through it, he sped up a stairway past a sign reading, *To Roof.*

Opening another door at the top of the flight of stairs, he emerged upon the roof and looked around. He saw nothing but the dome of the capitol looming in the distance.

"Vince?" he called, half whisper, half cry. Then, seeing and hearing nothing, he tried again. "Vince?"

Cautiously, becoming slightly nervous, he started across the roof toward a water tower. It was decrepit, ancient like the rest of the structure, looking as though even dust would leak from its bottom. "Vince?" he called. Then a little louder, "Hey, Vince?" He rounded the corner of the water tower and saw a man, at least his shoes, the bottom of his pants, the crown of his hat. The rest of him was masked by the *Washington Post.* The man lowered the paper, squinting up at the mask.

"I can't believe the Mets made this trade," he said in a tone of wounded sincerity that made it seem as though the maneuvering of baseball managers was, at this moment, the most important thing in his life. "What the hell do they need another pitcher for? That's all they got is pitchers."

16

Sighing in disbelief, Vince Ricardo rose, folded his paper, and came down the rusting steps of the water tower. He was in the later innings of his forties, a dark-haired, compact man who carried his head at a tilt as though he had achieved his full growth in a room with a very low ceiling.

"Why up here?" the man in the mask asked. "I don't understand."

"There's reasons," Vince answered. "I don't just do things. There's always a valid reason," he explained calmly, almost clinically, in his sincere tones. His head nodded toward the black bag. "Lemme see."

The masked man snapped the bag open and held it out for inspection. Vince looked inside, checking the contents, then nodded and took the bag. "Any problems?"

"None."

"Fabulous. Fabulous work." Vince's voice left no doubt that he thought the work was indeed fabulous. "Now, what's the story? Are you going to bill me or what?"

"He wants a million five for this," said the mouth behind the ski mask.

Vince waved casually. "No sweat," he said.

"By tomorrow."

"What?" Vince's crinkly eyes looked wounded.

"I'm sorry. That's what he told me," the mask apologized.

"But that's completely nuts! My kid's getting married on Sunday," Vince explained. "How the hell does he expect me to come up with that kind of money—"

"Vince—" the man began to interrupt.

"Do you know that I haven't even met the bride's

family yet?" Vince demanded. And, justifying himself, added, "That's how completely tied up I've been with this deal."

"Vince, if it was up to me," the other man replied, "you could take two weeks. But that's what he said." There was a slight emphasis on "he," not a threat but something that implied, Business is business and I'm just a messenger.

"Jesus Christ," Vince said with disgust. "Okay, I'll just have to work it out, that's all." He put out his hand and shook the masked man's, implying that he certainly had no hard feelings against him. "Thanks for everything. How's the wife?" Vince sounded like he really wanted to know.

"Fine. Her tennis is really coming along," the masked man answered.

"No kidding," Vince said, impressed. Then, philosophically, "You know, that's one game I could never get the hang of. I don't know what the hell it is. Maybe it's because you gotta wear short pants to play."

In the distance they could hear a siren begin to wail.

"Guess we oughta break this up," the man in the mask said regretfully.

"Yeah. Take it easy."

"You too, Vince." Abruptly the man in the mask turned and ran swiftly but silently back to the stairway door.

Vince hefted the battered black bag and turned too, walking in the opposite direction to the far end of the roof. There he scaled a small, low wall and landed on the roof of the adjacent building. Casually, he sauntered along that roof as though it were a boardwalk in Atlantic City, carrying the bag with the engravings, admiring, once again, the purity of style of the capitol dome and feeling proud to be an American.

3

Abe Hirschorn had never become accustomed to going to the dentist in an office building. Dentistry, he felt, was a homey occupation and should be practiced in a home. In a built-on extension to a nice clapboard house, jutting out into a backyard, where a person could look at a tree out the window while the dentist drilled. Since he lived in New York City he could even have accepted a dentist's office in the ground floor of a nice apartment building somewhere like Central Park West or Riverside Drive from which he could still see a tree through the window. But an office building? Every time he walked around the corner from Grand Central Station and into the twenties-style building where the dentist's office was, he felt like he should be there to sell slips and chemises, bed jackets and nightgowns, and that he had forgotten his sample case. But the sample case was long forgotten, for Abe Hirschorn at seventy-two had been retired for years.

He had this morning gotten out of the elevator at ten and walked down the long corridor to the door with the frosted-glass window and the words *Dr. Sheldon Korn-pett* written on it. He had entered the waiting room, sat down, and read half an article in *Newsweek*. Evita, Dr. Kornpett's round and cheerful Spanish nurse, had then escorted him into the inner office. It was modern and well equipped, a dental chair where the desk should have been. He sat in the chair and allowed Dr. Kornpett to swab his gum with something antiseptic. Then Kornpett took the huge syringe and as he plunged it into the old man's jaw, Abe thought, He's a nice-looking boy. What boy? He's gotta be at least mid-forties. When the dentists start look-ing like boys, Abe told himself, it means you're getting old.

Dr. Kornpett withdrew the needle, and Abe allowed Evita to return him to the waiting room while another patient took his place in the chair. By the time he finished the article in *Newsweek*, his nose was numb and he was back in the chair. Sheldon Kornpett, the boy dentist, had a wrench in his mouth and was ready to yank.

"Okay, here we go," Dr. Kornpett said. Sensing, rather than feeling the tension on his poor old tooth as the dentist began to pull, the old man rose with him like a hooked fish. "No. Don't fight me, Mr. Hirschorn!" the dentist ordered. "Stay in the chair."

Sheldon pulled harder on the tooth, feeling the sweat begin to rise around his hair line. Why not, I'm lifting a hundred and seventy pounds of patient, he thought, as Hirschorn came further out of the chair. Sighing, Sheldon Kornpett let go of the tooth and Mr. Hirschorn flopped back into the chair.

"I cannot work this way," he told his patient.

"Doc, it's seventy-two years I have this tooth. He don't want to die," the old man whined.

"Mr. Hirschorn, a tooth isn't a 'he.' It's nerves and enamel. The tooth is rotten," Sheldon said firmly, "so we're pulling it. No big deal, really."

"Seventy-two years," Mr. Hirschorn replied, not listening to the dentist, adrift in memories. "This tooth had steaks; this tooth had just beans when I was poor . . ."

"I understand—"

"This tooth lived through two world wars, through the Depression, through Hitler, through the Ed Sullivan show when it was still called *The Toast of the Town*."

Sheldon heard the telephone ring in the reception room and wondered if Hirschorn was going to back up his whole morning. "Mr. Hirschorn," he began again, but the old man seemed even more agitated.

"This tooth chewed on beautiful women," he said, "including a second cousin of Molly Picon."

Evita poked her head into the office. "Dr. Kornpett, your wife is on the line," she said.

Sheldon nodded. "I'll be there in a second." Looking down, he continued to his patient, "Mr. Hirschorn, your tooth has had a wonderful, colorful life, but now it's time to say goodbye."

The old man nodded. "I understand. But I wanted you to know what kind of tooth this was."

"It's been a truly great tooth," Sheldon told him. "I

feel honored to pull it out of your mouth, which I will do after this call." He dropped his instrument on the tray with more clatter than he intended and walked over to the wall phone and picked up the receiver. "Hi," he said. "How's it going? The tent up yet?"

At the other end of the line, Carol Kornpett was looking through the window of her Teaneck kitchen at several workmen mangling her well-kept lawn as they struggled to erect a green-and-white tent. "Almost," she said.

"Geez! I'm getting excited," her husband said from his office in the city.

Carol nodded her short-cut, red-haired head, adjusting her bangs, a look of wry amusement on her small, perky face. He's excited, she thought and I'm making coffee for seven workmen.

"Is Barbara home?" the voice on the phone asked.

Carol looked across the kitchen to her daughter, a ripe and anxious bride, looking far more like a knockout than she should in jeans and a T-shirt. "Yeah, she's here. Being very domestic."

Barbara looked up from the carrots she was scraping, waved at the phone and called, "Hi."

"She says, 'Hi,'" Carol informed the father of the bride.

"And remember the wine," Barbara reminded.

"And remember the wine," Carol relayed. "And not Beaujolais. Get something fancier. Saint-Emilion or even a good California."

"Oakville 1970 is great," Barbara announced.

"Julia Child here says Oakville 1970. When do you think you'll be home?"

Sheldon, in the office, looked at his watch, and Mr. Hirschorn heard him say, "Six-thirty the latest. Yeah . . . Is he definitely coming? . . . I'll believe it when I see it . . . Yeah . . . Yeah, I'm a little nervous, but happy. Definitely happy. I feel good about everything . . . Listen, I have someone here . . ."

About time he remembered, Hirschorn thought.

"I have to run." Sheldon smacked a kiss into the phone and said, "Me too." He hung up and turned back to Mr. Hirschorn. "My daughter's getting married on Sunday," he explained.

"No kidding! That's great, Doc. *Mazeltov*. A nice boy?"

"Wonderful. A second-year law student at Yale."

"And the parents?" Mr. Hirschorn asked.

"The mother is a lovely woman. The father, it's funny, he's a big consultant and he travels so much that we've never actually had a chance to meet him. Tonight's the first time; they're coming for dinner."

Mr. Hirschorn furrowed his brow and thought a minute. "Call it off," he said.

"Call what off?" Sheldon Kornpett sounded startled.

"The wedding," the old man said. "Call it off until you know the father."

The dentist smiled. "The wedding's Sunday. I don't think—"

"Call it off."

"Mr. Hirschorn, my daughter is marrying the son, not the father."

"The son is the acorn," Hirschorn intoned. "You gotta look at the tree. I been around a little, give a listen. By the way," he said, changing the subject, "here." He put something into the dentist's hand.

Sheldon looked at his hand and saw the molar. "Your tooth?"

"I pulled it while you were on the phone." Mr. Hirschorn rose and took off his bib. "You're a nice boy, you could hurt yourself pulling like that." He put an arm around the dentist's shoulder. "Now, do me a favor," he said in a fatherly manner.

"I can't call it off," Sheldon said politely. "This isn't nineteenth-century Minsk. It's twentieth-century Teaneck."

"Okey-doke," Hirschorn shrugged. "I hope I'm wrong. Best of luck to you. Forget I said anything."

"I'll try. It'll all be fine, I know." Sheldon smiled in spite of the little gray misgiving eating away like a cavity in his brain. "Now sit down or you're going to bleed all over your shirt."

The kitchen clock said four-thirty and the roast was gorgeous. It had been cut for Carol and her guests personally by the good, expensive butcher at the shop in town. Not for the Kornpetts a dowdy family roast hauled protesting in a plastic cover from the cold shelf at Safeway. Thirty minutes a pound at three hundred, Carol thought, would be three and a half hours which means eight, which allows an hour for cocktails and chatter. Unless they're late. Or I could, she equivocated, try that other crazy way. Half an hour at five hundred and then turn off the oven and just leave it there, although you're not supposed to peek and that makes me nervous. Either way, if I start now, it's eight o'clock. But what if they're late? Or if they cancel? Tommy was a sweet boy but his father had to be called unreliable, even if she hadn't met him. As a matter of fact, that was why she thought of him as unreliable. It was not too late to take the roast from the roasting pan and freeze it for the next scheduled dinner if they were canceling. Except, the next scheduled dinner then could only be after the wedding.

Oh God! she thought and looked at the clock. Four thirty-five.

"It's too beautiful to waste on just us," she said, although there was no one else in the kitchen. Barbara was having an extended bath. Resolutely, Carol moved to the kitchen phone and, leafing through the little directory she kept beside it, found the number and dialed. She heard the clickety-buzz of the ringing instrument, and after three combinations it was picked up and she heard the voice of Barbara's future mother-in-law.

"Hello?"

"Jean, it's Carol," she said and gave the silly little laugh she had decided upon but not rehearsed. It sounded very phony. "Listen, I couldn't remember, did I say seven or eight?"

"Seven," Jean answered. "Is that too early?"

"Oh, no. It simply doesn't matter," Carol assured her. "I just wanted to be sure because I was putting in my roast."

"Oh, I hope you haven't gone to a lot of trouble." Jean Ricardo knew her cues and her dialogue in this kind of conversation.

"Oh, no. Just a simple family dinner," Carol cooed, figuring hastily forty dollars worth if you count the shrimp cocktail. "So you and Vince and Tommy will be here at seven . . ."

27

"We're looking forward to it. Vince especially," Jean answered.

"Barbara mentioned Tommy said Vince was away yesterday," Carol said, getting to the nitty-gritty.

"Oh, he'll be back," Jean fairly sang into the phone.

"He isn't there yet?" Carol asked a trifle nervously.

"You know Vince," Jean said with a little laugh.

"No, I don't," Carol answered.

"Well, you know what I mean," his wife answered, and both ladies laughed, knowing exactly what the other meant. "But he called. He's on his way."

"Oh, I'm so relieved," Carol said. "Shel and I are so anxious to get to know him."

"Him, too," Jean said.

"So I'll see you at seven?"

"On the dot," Jean said, and hung up. She turned toward Tommy, who had just wandered into the living room. "Your mother-in-law was afraid we wouldn't show and she'd blow her roast," she told him.

Feeling she'd done all she could humanly do, Carol slid the roast into the oven at three hundred. The other way made her nervous, and better safe than sorry. She decided not to tell Barbara she'd phoned.

She began to peel potatoes, glancing at the clock, which now said four forty-two. Plus three and a half is seven seventy-two, Carol figured, which is eight-twelve, which leaves an hour and twelve minutes for hanging up the coats and cocktails and the deviled eggs and conversation. I hope they don't like the roast too rare, she thought.

28

4

The sound of the car could be heard at some distance on the quiet suburban street. A man's figure appeared in the downstairs window of the handsome two-story colonial house, hunched forward, trying to see if this was the car he waited for. Ignoring the crushed hopes of the figure in the French window, the car sailed majestically past the colonial, the window, the man, and on down the street.

In the elegantly furnished living room of the house, Sheldon Kornpett allowed the curtain and the drape to fall back and moved from the window to the fireplace. "False alarm," he said.

"I hope they didn't have an accident," Carol Kornpett

said, allowing her tardy guests every courtesy. She sat, hostess-nervous, as though her armchair were actually a bed of nails. She wore a sleekly tailored blouse and a long dark skirt, striking just the proper note between "dressed up" and "at home."

"I know Mr. Ricardo's been out of town," Barbara said from the couch opposite the fireplace. "He might've gotten hung up."

"Hung up," her father muttered angrily.

Carol rose. "I have to take that roast beef out of the oven."

"Just keep it on the warmer," Barbara advised.

"I'll try," Carol said, her tone reminding her daughter she'd been warming roasts for years. She walked past the well-stocked built-in bar, up the few steps to the entrance hall, and out to the kitchen. Sheldon stalked back to the window.

"This is a great start," he said. "One hour late."

"I'm sure there's a good reason."

"They could've called."

"If the traffic was bad, they couldn't call—"

Sheldon whirled on his daughter. "Why are you taking their side?"

"I'm not taking anybody's side," Barbara said defensively.

"You're still in our family," he reminded her.

"Oh, God, Dad. Don't lay this on me. They're late. All right. Don't make a family issue."

"He's such a hotshot, how come he doesn't have a phone in the car?"

"Who said he was a hotshot?"

"You did," Sheldon snapped. "He travels all over the

30

place. He's so busy." He hit the word as though it were an ill-fitting bridge. "It's unbelievable we've never met him. I had a guy in the office today, Mr. Hirschorn, said I should call the whole thing off."

"That's a brilliant solution to the problem," his daughter said sharply.

Suddenly a glare of light entered the window and circled the room and they heard the sound of tires on gravel. The father of the bride looked anxiously out of the window, "A Coupe de Ville?" he asked.

"That's them," Barbara said. "Are you okay, Dad, or are you going to be totally hostile to them? If you are . . ."

"Don't worry, I'll be fine," Sheldon said with a certain stony grandeur. He headed for the entrance hall. Barbara followed him, and Carol, hearing the bell, came back from the kitchen just in case Sheldon wasn't "fine."

In front of the open door the Ricardo family were framed in the porch light looking like a late-mailed Christmas card. The father, a short, dark man, stood beside his wife, Jean, a petite blond woman. Tommy hovered behind them.

Vince Ricardo smiled his most ingratiating smile and in his sincerest manner asked, "Will you ever forgive me?"

Sheldon pulled himself together with a massive effort and smiled. The Ricardos came into the entrance hall and were greeted by all three Kornpetts. Tommy, as he hugged his bride-to-be, shook his head in exasperation and offered, by way of explanation, "Dad, of course."

"It's all my fault," Vince trumpeted, *mea culpa* style, over the greetings. "I had business in Montreal and those damn Canadians just never stop talking." He turned from this general expression of apology to his hostess. "You must be the lovely mother of the bride."

"I am," Carol said, seeing no point in denying it.

"Now I know where Barbara gets her looks," Vince said. He kissed her.

"Hello, folks," Jean Ricardo said. "Count on Vince." She apologized and exonerated herself in one small phrase.

"We're just glad you're here," Sheldon said, and kissed Jean. He held out his hand to Vince. "I'm Sheldon Korn-pett."

"Well, Shelley, I'm just thrilled to meet you. Tommy tells me you were the first dentist ever to use that drill which spritzes water."

Sheldon nodded, pleased. Evidently Vince had struck the right note. "Among the first in New York, I think," he said modestly and waited a moment for further congratulations. When none came, he continued, "Please, what are we standing around for? Let's have a drink."

"I could really use one," Vince said gratefully. "What a day. Shelley, have you ever had one of those days . . ."

"You do consulting work, is that right?" Sheldon asked as they all started moving toward the living room.

Carol, torn between graciousness and a ruined dinner, interrupted. "People, I hate to say this, but if we don't sit down and eat, that roast beef is going to be inedible."

"Well, I'm starving, so it's fine with me," Vince announced.

"Don't stand on formalities with us," his wife added.

Sheldon pointed to the dining room. "This way, please," he said, and shepherded the Ricardos in.

Behind them in the entrance hall, Tommy whispered to Barbara, "I'm really petrified."

"My father was like a maniac before you came," she answered.

Carol went back into the kitchen and got the shrimp cocktails out of the refrigerator. As she placed them on the tray, she looked over at the roast on the warmer and wondered if somewhere, deep in the middle, there might be the slightest hint of pink.

Valiantly, Carol hacked away at the slice of beef on her plate. She had selected the most overdone piece for herself although it had been difficult to decide which one that was. "Vince, how long did you actually live in Guatemala?" she asked, hostess-bright. Relative calm had settled over the dining room and everyone had tactfully avoided mentioning the food.

"He was gone for ages," Jean Ricardo said as her husband swallowed.

"I was in the jungle—the bush, we call it—for approximately nine months," Vince said.

Sheldon looked up. "That must have been something."

"Shelley, it was unbelievable. I saw things . . . they had tsetse flies down there the size of eagles . . . really," Vince said as though someone might doubt him. "In the evenings I would stand in front of my hut and watch in horror as these giant flies picked children up off the ground and carried them off."

"My God," Carol gasped.

"He told us things . . ." Jean allowed the sentence to trail off as though the things were much too horrible to repeat in Teaneck.

"An incredible sight." Vince nodded his head, remembering. "The peasants screaming, chasing these flies down the road, waving brooms . . . Can you imagine the pathetic quality of this? . . . Waving crudely fashioned brooms at these enormous flies as they carried their children off to certain death."

Sheldon looked as though he couldn't imagine it at all, but Carol was transfixed. "That's the most horrible—" she began, but her literal-minded husband cut her off.

"You sure these are flies you're talking about?" Sheldon asked.

Vince nodded. "Flies. The natives have a name for them: *joségrecos de muertos*. Flamenco dancers of death."

"You took those slides of them that never came out," his wife reminded him.

"That's a shame," Sheldon said. "I would have loved to see them."

"I left them in a jacket that got Martinized," Vince regretted. "I'll tell you, it broke my heart, because those slides would have won me a Pulitzer Prize. The enormous flies flapping slowly away into the sunset, the small brown children clutched in their beaks."

"Wow," Barbara mumbled in awe.

"Their beaks?" her father asked, a peculiar expression on his face. "Flies with beaks?"

"A sight I will never forget. I was stunned, appalled . . ."

"What did you do?" Carol asked.

Vince looked at her. "What did I do?"

"As a consultant, I mean," she answered. "About the flies."

Vince looked unhappy. "Sadly, there was very little I could do, because of the tremendous red tape in the bush."

"There's red tape in the bush?" Sheldon asked sharply.

"Enormous red tape. Those flies, for instance, are protected from pilferage under the provisions of the Guacamole Act of 1917."

Barbara shot a look at her intended, who just rolled his eyes. Her father was saying, "It's amazing. I've gotten the *National Geographic* for years; I never heard about—"

Barbara decided it was time to say, "Could I have a little more wine?"

"Of course," Carol said.

"I'd love some, too," Vince said, and as Carol filled his glass, he continued, "for the purpose of a toast."

"What a good idea!" Jean beamed her approval.

"I'm not the most eloquent guy in the world," Vince began, "but I would like to say that this has been a most lovely occasion . . ."

"I couldn't agree more," Jean slid in her endorsement under her husband's oration.

". . . and on Sunday," he continued, "we'll have another occasion, even more lovely, more sacred . . ."

As his voice droned on, Sheldon saw the man's figure begin to ripple, to slide in and out of focus. The dentist realized that his eyes were filling with tears.

". . . and all I really want to say—and I know Jean and Tommy go along with me—is that I'm just honored and moved to become part of the Kornpett family, and I hope we'll be together in the good times to share them

35

with joy, and if there's bad times, God forbid, that we'll work that out, too. But together."

Barbara looked up from her hands, which were entwined in Tommy's. "That was really very lovely, Mr. Ricardo," she said.

"I feel the same way, Dad," her fiancé echoed.

Sheldon rose, feeling almost unable to speak but knowing he had to. He picked up his wineglass and said, "Well, hard as it is to give my little girl away . . ." A tear rolled down his cheek. ". . . I'm glad that I'm giving her away to someone as fine as Tommy. And I hope the Kornpetts and the Ricardos will share many happy and peaceful occasions for . . ." He felt suddenly as though he had painted himself into a corner. Unable to find the graceful phrase that would get him out, he finished, a bit lamely, with "many happy and peaceful years."

Struggling through the miasma of sentiment that blanketed her like smog, Carol managed to cry, "Hear! Hear!" as Barbara rushed to her father, put her arms around him and told him, "Oh, Dad, that was sweet!"

The Kornpett family's tears were like a gentle summer mist surrounding all three, and Jean Ricardo's empathetic reaction was stronger still, a spring shower of sensitivity. Vince, however, was a veritable hurricane of emotion . . . a downpour of tears accompanied by thunderclaps of sobs he vainly tried to stanch with his napkin. Tommy, alone at one end of the table, felt uncomfortably unable to rise to the occasion and stared at his father.

Sobbing, Vince lowered the napkin from his streaming eyes and checked his watch. Abruptly, he stopped crying and said, in a most businesslike way, "Excuse me, where's the phone?"

Sheldon, professionally accustomed to tears in his office, was startled by Vince's mercurial switch in mood. "Phone?" he asked, to be sure he had heard correctly.

"There's one in the kitchen," Carol said, somewhat more composed by now.

"Where's the farthest one?" Vince asked. "I gotta call long distance and sometimes, with these overseas connections, I gotta scream like a banshee."

"There's one in the basement, but it's a mess," his host told him.

"That's okay," Vince answered, and pointed to the kitchen. "Through there?"

Carol rose and said, "I'll show you."

"Please don't bother. I'll find it." Vince started for the kitchen door.

Tommy smiled. "Dad and his mysterious phone calls," he said.

His father stopped in his tracks, the look he gave his son, the tone of his voice pure ice. "What did you say?"

Tommy's smile faded. "I just said, you and your mysterious phone calls."

"What the hell do you mean by that?" Vince sounded dangerously as though he were restraining himself.

"Nothing, really. You're just always making those weird phone calls in back rooms and pay booths."

Vince's fury broke through. "You little snotnose!" he yelled. "Those phone calls put you through college."

"Vince . . ." his wife called. The single syllable was a warning, a reminder of where he was, and a plea, all blended in one.

Of the astonished Kornpetts only Barbara could pull herself together enough to say, "I'm sure Tommy didn't mean—"

But her father-in-law-to-be cut her off. "I fight my way up to a position where I'm making these kind of high-quality phone calls to top businessmen and my own son derogates—"

"Dad, I wasn't derogating," his son interrupted in turn.

Suddenly Vince's head of steam dissipated like a kettle taken from the burner. "Maybe you weren't," he said, calmly. "I'm terribly sorry, everybody. It's been a long day." He pointed to the kitchen again. "This way?"

"It's the door in the kitchen," Sheldon told him. "Pull a string for light."

"Thanks a billion," Vince said and left the dining room.

There was a symphony of throat-clearing behind him. When the embarrassed phlegm was gone, Jean Ricardo said, "He's been working so hard recently. Normally—"

"Listen—" Sheldon said, trying to forestall her apology.

Barbara told her parents, "He's usually so affectionate with Tommy. So physical—"

"Listen, I can understand a certain amount of resentment," her fiancé broke in. "He's had a hard life. I really haven't."

Everyone nodded in agreement or relief.

In the kitchen, Vince opened the door to the cellar stairs. Seeing a switch inside, he turned on the bare bulb and started down, carefully closing the door behind him. Reaching the bottom step, he pulled a dangling chain, and the light revealed a musty, unfinished basement.

Across the cement floor he saw a workbench. There was not much else to see, a few boxes, a suitcase, the sort of elderly possessions people dump into a basement because they are unable or unwilling to part with them. Seeing the phone, he crossed the room, wondering why the Kornpetts had never finished off the basement—some paneling, a Ping-Pong table, he thought. The kind of money a dentist pulls in, one gold crown alone . . .

Pushing the thought away, he lifted the receiver and dialed a number. Hearing the receiver lifted, he said, "It's Ricardo." Then, in answer to a question, "Yes, very smoothly, but listen, it's impossible, that kind of money by tomorrow . . ." He listened for a moment, interrupting the voice on the wire to say, "No, you don't understand; this is a major international deal. It's not like we're fencing some shit on the street." There was a long and possibly angry answer from the other side of the wire. "No," Vince said, "they're not all in there. I held onto one in case you pulled something like—" His voice was rising, his eyes scanning the dim room with some concern in them. "What's the point in threatening me?" he asked the phone. "You can't—" And, hearing a click, "Hello?" Then he muttered, "Christ!" when there was no reply, and hung up, clearly disturbed.

Vince stood for a moment, thinking, then, fishing into his pocket, pulled out the five-hundred-dollar-bill engraving. He looked around the unpromising basement, then moved quickly to a brick wall near the phone. Touching the wall in the dim light, he felt around for a loose brick. Finding one, he tugged it out of the wall, thanking God or whoever was responsible that the Kornpetts had been too cheap or too unimaginative to panel the basement. Holding the brick, he placed the plate in the cavity, then carefully replaced the brick. He looked over to the workbench and, seeing what he wanted, moved to it and picked up a piece of chalk. Then he went back to the wall and marked the brick as inconspicuously as possible. Tossing the chalk back to the worktable, he crossed the room to the stairs and pulled the string on the bulb. Arranging a smile on his face, he started back up the cellar stairs.

As their parents said good night in the entrance hall, Barbara maneuvered Tommy through the door and down the walk to the relative privacy beside his father's car.

The evening had been pleasant after Vince's outburst. The parents and Barbara had sat over dessert in the dining room and over liqueurs in the living room and some had talked and others had answered just like real people. True, her father had seemed a bit tense, but it was not active hostility, and Barbara had decided to put his behavior down to nerves. Only Tommy had seemed to withdraw, sitting quietly beside Barbara on the sofa, rarely speaking unless directly spoken to. As she listened to the others and even as she spoke herself, Barbara considered her fiancé. She had never seen his father behave like that to him, had suddenly gotten a picture of a childhood that might, perhaps, have not been quite as easy, as loving, as her own. Within these thoughts came the seeds of guilt. She loved Tommy, and her refusal last night, she realized now, was mean-spirited and stupid. And capricious. He, poor lamb, might have been sitting on the sofa beside her thinking he was marrying into a situation of unexplained acceptances and mystifying rejections just like the situation he was marrying out of. She had resolved to make it up to him, and here, now, beside the car, she implemented her decision by kissing him.

"Tomorrow . . ." she whispered. It was both an invitation and an acceptance.

"Tomorrow what?" Tommy asked.

"Tomorrow night," she clarified.

"Oh, of course," he answered, but not with enough enthusiasm for her to feel that she had made herself clear. "I thought you might be busy," Tommy continued. "Y'know . . . the preparations . . . food . . . ironing things . . ." he said vaguely.

His parents were out of the door now, completing their adieus on the front step. "I mean the motel," Barbara whispered and was pleased to see him perk up for the first time since Vince's dressing down.

"Terrific," he said. "I'll pick you up at nine and talk about a movie in front of your folks."

By then his parents and hers had joined them. Barbara's quick peck good-night kiss to Tommy was no more emotional than the duty pecks she gave his parents.

No matter what crisis the day might have brought, Sheldon Kornpett invariably brushed his teeth before retiring. As a professional man he felt it was the least he could do. Now, staring at himself in the mirror wearing the long, dark Oriental robe Carol had given him for his birthday, he brushed furiously, viciously, hard enough to scratch the enamel.

"What are you talking about, Dad?" Barbara asked from the open bathroom door.

Sheldon whirled around, gums raw, toothpaste smeared

41

across his lips. "What am I talking about? He's crazy! That's what I'm talking about."

So it's hostility, Barbara decided, and attacked as the best defense. "He's crazy?" She emphasized the pronoun. "Look at yourself. You're foaming at the mouth."

"It's toothpaste," he said and wiped it off with a towel. "Barbara, I love you dearly, but I've been around a little longer than you. The man is unstable. I don't want you marrying into that family."

"You're being absolutely Sicilian about this. I'm marrying Tommy, not Vince."

A vision of his patient, old man Hirschorn, swam before Sheldon's eyes. "He's the acorn," he said.

"Who's the acorn? What acorn?"

Too upset to remember exactly how Hirschorn had phrased it, Sheldon muttered, "It's a saying," and stalked past Barbara out of the bathroom and down the hall.

She followed him. "It's a great saying, Dad. Really captures a whole lot."

"Spare me the sarcasm, will you?" her father yelled. "I'm telling you, it's off." He stormed into the bedroom but the girl followed.

"It is not off!"

"It is off!"

Carol, at her vanity table removing her makeup, peered at them through cold-creamed eyelashes.

"We'll call the caterers, call the guests. An expensive mistake, that's all, but not as bad as marrying into that crazy family."

Furious and desperate, Barbara yelled, "Goddammit, you will not call it off. Tommy and I will go to Vegas or some sleazy thing like that. I don't care. But we are getting married. Mom, for God's sakes, will you tell him?"

Trying to sound rational, Carol said, "Shelley, you're really being quite irrational."

"I'm being irrational?" he yelled. "I sit there listening to these cockamamie stories about giant tsetse flies and the Guacamole Act of 1917 and I'm irrational?"

"So he embellishes—" Carol minimized.

"He's a crazy person! He's laughing, then he's crying, then he practically slugs Tommy in the mouth—"

"He didn't practically slug—" his daughter began.

"He has to go into the basement to make a phone call to God knows where . . ." Running out of accusations, Sheldon's voice trailed off.

"And what else?" Barbara asked calmly.

"His whole manner."

"And for that you want to call off the wedding?"

"Shelley," Carol interposed.

"I just don't like it," he said.

"You're just projecting like crazy," his daughter told him.

"Here we go. Psychology on Parade," her father announced.

"Let her talk, Shelley," Carol advised.

"It's not easy for fathers to give away daughters," the girl began. "It's a complicated relationship. There's sexual stuff going on . . ."

"Hey!" her father interrupted angrily.

"I'm not talking about incest, for chrissake, but there is a certain sexual component to father-daughter relationships. So the closer the wedding gets, I think the more edgy you're going to be and you're going to fix on things like Mr. Ricardo being a little flaky—which I'm not denying—as a reason to reject the whole idea of marriage."

Carol said, "I think she's right."

"Five thousand a year tuition so I can listen to that!" the father stormed.

"It doesn't make sense?" Barbara asked sensibly.

Sheldon sighed, smiled wanly, walked to his daughter, and hugged her somewhat tearily. "It makes sense. You're a smart cookie." He kissed the girl and, walking to his wife at the vanity table, kissed her for good measure. "I'm sorry," he said.

"There's no reason to be sorry," Barbara said. "The only thing I want is that you be more open to Tommy's father. Don't just reject him."

"I won't. I'll make a real effort."

"Imagine how nervous he was tonight, Shel, meeting you."

"Tommy's told him so much about you," Barbara said, bolstering her mother's argument.

Sheldon nodded. "Well, he *was* nervous," he said, the subtle flattery getting to him.

"Sure he was," Carol chimed in.

"Okay," the husand-father-dentist-almost-in-law said and smiled. "Finished," he wiped it up. "I'll do my best. I'll just be incredibly receptive," he promised.

5

Eighth Avenue is perhaps the most schizophrenic thoroughfare in New York, a city famous for the chameleonlike quality of its neighborhoods. Rooted insecurely in the northern reaches of Greenwich Village, it skitters uptown past relatively modern housing developments, the General Post Office, Macy's, and into the garment district. At Fortieth Street it descends before the Port Authority Bus Terminal into a world of instant sleaziness. The forties and fifties along Eighth Avenue bring a new meaning to the words "urban blight." Bars and massage parlors stand hunched beside porno movie houses which improve the city's cultural tone by unreeling hetero- and homosexual sagas in sixteen millimeters enlivened by stage shows featuring, as the case may be, nubile, undressed dancing boys or couples looking unwashed and un-erotic "doing it." At Columbus Circle, the avenue curves around a statue of The Man Who Made It All Possible and is reborn into elegant and expensive Central Park West. Then it flows into the far reaches of Harlem. But these areas need not concern us.

Back in the mid-forties, two large men lurk in front of an ancient office building. The sight of Angie and Mo in a dark alley would be enough to give the strongest heart a cardiac arrest; but even in daylight they are sinister. They stand near the doorway of the building, observing through puffed and beady eyes the light flow of traffic, the sprinkling of pedestrians. They are conspicuous in the early morning, for Eighth Avenue is a nighttime neighborhood. They are here on business, and their business, for the moment, is to wait.

Inside a cab hurtling up the avenue, Vince Ricardo leaned forward to call through the antimugging sheet of plexiglass, "My building's on the next corner." As the cab slowed down, looking through the window, Vince saw the two large men and mumbled, "Christ!" Then he called, "Keep going," to the young cabbie.

The cabbie seemed to take that as a personal insult. "That's 721, man," he said.

"I said keep going," Vince repeated, his tone allowing for no argument. The cab sped past the building. Angie and Mo, innocent of the fact that their quarry had seen them (if of nothing else), continued their vigil in the filth.

"Stupid goddamn bastards!" Vince muttered, pale and agitated.

"Any particular place you want me to go?" the driver

asked with the resigned sarcasm of an experienced New York cabbie.

Vince flipped quickly through the Rollerdex of possible destinations in his mind, and finding one, took out his wallet and removed the business card Sheldon Kornpett had given him. "Three forty-two Madison Avenue," he read to the cabbie, "pronto."

"Then pronto it will be," the cabbie answered with exaggerated efficiency and took the corner of the next eastbound street on two wheels.

Mrs. Adelman's mouth was open, which was not unusual. That she did not take advantage of an open mouth to speak, was. Her eyes were firmly closed, as she preferred not knowing what was happening in the dentist's chair. To get her mind off the horrors to which Dr. Kornpett might be subjecting her, she was concentrating on remembering the words to "The Star-Spangled Banner." She had already gone through "My Country 'Tis of Thee," and a pretty good facsimile of the Pledge of Allegiance.

Now, sensing a momentary pause, she risked a quick look. Dr. Kornpett hovered above her, seen from the nasal-hair angle. Beside him, slightly out of focus, Mrs. Adelman felt the white, starched presence of Evita.

"A number six," she heard Dr. Kornpett say, and Evita handed him a silver instrument. "Thank you," he said and turned his attention to his patient. "We're looking good, Mrs. Adelman."

"Awwfffmm," she replied.

"No. Probably another two visits after this one," he replied, and she wondered whether dentists took a class in understanding impeded speech. "Scraper," the dentist directed to Evita, and just as she reclosed her eyes, frightened by the connotation of the word, Mrs. Adelman thought she saw a third head appear between the doctor and his nurse.

"A number four," Sheldon said, and as Evita handed it to him, Vince leaned between them to get a better view of Sheldon's work.

"I'm watching a master at work," he said humbly.

The dentist screamed. Mrs. Adelman concentrated fiercely on whether "the rockets' red glare," came before or after "the bombs bursting in sight."

"Vince!" Sheldon yelled, whirling in fright.

"Out of the office, please," Evita ordered. Whether the intruder was a friend or a drug addict, there was a patient in the chair.

"Did I startle you folks?" Vince asked innocently.

Sheldon massaged his chest, reassuring his heart. "You really did, Vince," he answered.

"Please, out of the office!"

"It's okay, Evita," the dentist said.

"Evita?" Vince repeated. "I'm delighted to meet you." He offered her his hand. "I'm Vince Ricardo. Dr. Kornpett's wonderful daughter is marrying my son."

Unable to decide whether good manners were more important than medical protocol, Evita split the difference, said nothing, and shook hands with Vince. The dentist said, "Vince," again. Mrs. Adelman, deciding that the bombs burst in air rather than in sight, opened her eyes again. She was looking at a short, dark man.

"Hello, dear," he said. "This is some great dentist you've got here. You're a very lucky woman."

48

"Mmpfilggr," she replied.

The man said, "No kidding," but Mrs. Adelman didn't think he had really understood her.

"Vince . . ." Dr. Kornpett said, rather more firmly.

"I'm on my way. I was just in the neighborhood, thought I'd stop up and say howdy-do."

"That's very nice. If you have a minute, we could talk while this sets."

"I don't want to intrude," the intruder said.

Dr. Kornpett smiled, but Mrs. Adelman didn't think he was too happy. "No bother at all," he told the man, and turned to her. "Now, don't move your head if at all possible," he told her, "and keep your mouth open for five minutes. Okay?"

"Awwrlllmm."

The dentist said, "Fine," and the strange man added, "Listen to the doc now." He patted her arm. "You're very sweet," he said, and somewhere behind her, probably at the door, she heard the doctor say, "Vince," again and they left her alone. She decided to think about the strange man and go back to "The Star-Spangled Banner" when the dentist returned.

"That's a wonderful patient you've got there," Vince told Sheldon. They were in a small corridor. "Very fine woman."

"You know her?" Sheldon asked.

"No. But I could tell she was a person of real quality."

Sheldon opened the door to his private office and gestured for Vince to enter.

"The inner sanctum, huh?" Vince asked and, going through the door, continued, "Remember that show on the radio, *Inner Sanctum?*"

"Sure."

"I never missed it." Sheldon went to his desk. He saw that Vince was examining the framed certificates and diplomas on the wall of the small room.

"You understand Latin?" his guest asked.

"Just a little."

"You know what all this means?"

"It means they won't arrest me for impersonating a dentist." Vince laughed uproariously. Sheldon, knowing it was not that funny, wondered what the hell his almost in-law wanted.

"Very funny," Vince was still chuckling. "Impersonating a dentist. That's real cute."

What is with this guy, Sheldon wondered. And how do I get rid of him? It's obviously up to me to say something. "Nice of you to stop by," he tried.

"Well, I figure we're practically family now. I like to feel close."

"Listen, any time you're in the neighborhood . . ." Sheldon hoped that that was a stronger hint.

"That's very kind of you, Shel." Vince sat down, settling in. "And don't think I'll abuse the privilege. I'm not one of these guys who, you give 'em an inch . . ."

"Any time," Sheldon said. He thought, If he's going to take a yard, how long will he take to take it?

"That's wonderful, but I can see how busy you are here. The waiting room's filled."

Sheldon nodded, pleased, beginning to see some light at the end of the tunnel of this visit. "It's a very good practice," he admitted.

"Looks like an absolute gold mine. You're hopping all the time, huh? I mean, if I asked you to leave the office for a couple of minutes, that wouldn't be possible, would it?"

Sheldon shrugged. "That would depend."

"What about right now?" Vince asked.

With a sinking feeling the dentist realized his guest did have a purpose, however murkily disguised. "Right now what?"

"Could I borrow you for a couple of minutes?"

"Now?"

"Would it be terribly inconvenient?" Vince asked seriously. "Please tell me if it is. I just thought, 'cause it was around lunch time . . ."

"Lunch time?" Sheldon checked his digital watch, sure, no matter how it felt, that Vince could not have been there that long. "It's a quarter past nine," he said.

"You never take an early lunch?"

"I don't take a real lunch. I work straight through."

Vince smiled. "So there's no problem."

About what? Sheldon wondered. And, feeling he had to get the man to the point, whatever it might be, said, "Vince, I've got patients waiting. What exactly do you want?"

"It's such a minor thing . . ." Vince looked almost ashamed at having brought it up. "I'm almost embarrassed to ask, but I just need a hand for maybe five minutes tops."

Sheldon hesitated. "Five minutes?"

"At the most. I got a cab waiting downstairs."

"I hate to turn you down," Sheldon said, "but I've got two impacted molars and a gold crown sitting out there. I'm all backed up."

"Listen . . . what the hell, I can do it myself. You're so busy . . ."

But the man did look disappointed and Sheldon felt like a crumb. "I could do it this evening. Around five-thirty," he offered.

"No, I'll manage. I don't want to make a federal case out of this."

The thought of the two families getting off on the wrong foot and impairing his daughter's happiness was balanced against the molars and the gold crown. "It's really important to you?" Sheldon asked, trying to weigh all sides.

"It would be so helpful, you can't imagine," Vince said sincerely. "Like I say, it's no big deal . . ."

What the hell? Sheldon thought, and said, "You know what? I never get out of this place." He stood up. What's five minutes for a member of the family?"

Vince rose, beaming. "Oh, Shel, this is just stupendously nice of you. And you might even enjoy it."

"Where are we going?"

"Just over to my office," Vince said. "I want you to break into my safe."

Rubin's Catering Service's estimate for the reception had actually been rather high, but Carol's friend Bunny had told her that after Bunny's son's bar mitzvah they had actually deducted for some unopened champagne and freezer-wrapped the leftover hors d'oeuvres. So Carol had engaged them. So far, she was very pleased. At least the men that worked for Rubin's were neat, cheerful, and had not smashed into any furniture carrying the heavy crates of soda through the house and down into the basement.

"Why don't you just stack them against that wall?" she suggested. "It's close to the stairs."

"Fine," one of them said, and he and his companion moved across the basement.

"Day after tomorrow, huh, Mrs. Kornpett?" the other one said.

Carol made a face. "God, don't remind me. There's so much to do."

"Anything we can do, feel free to call us," the first one said, as they started stacking the soda.

"That's really very sweet of you," Carol said, and, "Whoops!" as a loose brick came tumbling out of the wall.

"Geez. I'm sorry," the second man said.

"It's okay," she reassured him. "That brick comes out all the time. One day we're going to get sued."

The man nodded and picked up the brick. Carol watched as he started to replace it, then heard him say, "Hey!"

"What?" she asked.

He pulled something from the hole and stared at it. The other man looking over his shoulder told Carol, "An engraving."

"For a five hundred," his friend amplified.

"A what?" Carol asked and went over to look. Never having seen anything like it before, it didn't mean much. "What did you say this was?" she asked.

"Looks like an engraving for a bill," the first man said. " 'United States of America,' see?"

"Maybe it's from the previous owners or something," the other man suggested.

"I doubt it. We've been here fifteen years."

"No. It looks new," the first man said.

"Isn't that the damnedest thing?" Carol said, wrinkling up her face. "Right in the cellar."

"People find all kinds of things in the cellar." The man said it as though he didn't want her to feel he thought she kept a sloppy house.

"I just can't imagine . . . what do you think I should do with this?"

The second man shrugged. "I've never seen one of them," he said.

"Take it to the bank. They'll know," the first man, who seemed to have the authority of leadership, told her.

"You think so?" Carol asked, considering the million things left to do.

"Sure," he said.

"You're probably right." She checked her watch, knowing she'd never get everything done and thinking, now this! "Maybe I can get there before noon," she said, deciding it was her duty as a citizen even if Barbara was getting married Sunday.

"I hate white shoes," Barbara said and stared out of the side window of the Toyota at one of the more commercial and more depressing sections of Bergen County.

"White shoes," Carol said, her mouth compressing firmly. She knew she ought to have bought them for Barbara herself, whether they fit or not, and avoided the argument.

"But I'll never be able to wear them again," Barbara whined. "It's wasting money." This was an argument that almost always had worked in the past.

"I have to go to the bank," Carol said, annoyed enough about the engraving in her purse, the extra errand when there was so much to do. "While I am there, you will go into the shoe store and buy a pair of white shoes for the wedding."

"I hate that shoe store," Barbara said. "Any shoe store that can call itself Old Mother Hubbard's is just too adorable to patronize."

"Don't quibble," Carol said, hardly moving her lips.

"If I got white sandals maybe I could stand to wear them with slacks or something in the summer."

"Pumps!" Carol spat out the word. She pulled the car into the exit of the shopping center parking lot, which was nearer to the bank than the entrance.

"Where is it written—" Barbara began, then screamed as her mother slammed on the brakes in front of a Peugeot that was dashing toward the exit.

"Damn!" Carol muttered and backed up a little to allow the enraged woman in the Peugeot to go around her, at the same time causing excessive honking from a Dodge Dart behind her. "You, too!" she called in answer to a suggestion the Peugeot driver made as she passed. Carol switched back into drive and plunged her car into the massed ranks in the parking lot. "It is written in the book of my good taste that with a white wedding gown, a bride wears white pumps," she told her daughter in no uncertain terms.

"You're being mid-Victorian!"

"Nevertheless," Carol answered as she slid into a parking place, "you are still my child, you are still living under my roof, and you will wear white shoes. Once you're married, you can wear whatever colored shoes you want to your wedding!" Snatching up her purse, she got out of the car and slammed the door.

From the opposite side, over the roof of the Toyota, Barbara said, "Maybe those colorless plastic—?"

"White!" Carol screamed and, turning on her heel, headed toward the bank, her purse heavier than usual with the inexplicable engraving inside it.

6

The cab hurtled up Eighth Avenue, a swerving, spinning broken-end run between the buses, trucks, and other quarterback-maneuvering cabs. It was later now, the traffic heavier, the morning shift of sidewalk hustlers, male, female, and what-the-hell-is-that? had already begun their day-long commercial strolls.

Sheldon sat wide-eyed in the back of the cab, the picture of a catatonic dentist in his white half-smock. Beside him, Vince was oblivious, lost in private thoughts, or dreams, or machinations. The cab screamed around a corner and came to an abrupt stop in front of the Emerald Isle Bar and Grill. The young cabbie leaned back and said, "The eagle has landed. What now?"

"Put your flashers on and stay put," Vince told him.

"Are we still moving?" Sheldon asked.

"No," Vince told him. "The cab stopped. We're on West Forty-sixth Street."

"Did we hit that little boy on Sixth Avenue?" Sheldon asked.

"No. We missed him by a good foot and a half," Vince reassured him. "Okay, now . . ." He took a slip of paper and a key from his pocket and handed them to Sheldon. "This opens the office door," he said, "and this is the combination to the safe."

Sheldon took the key and the paper and examined them. Making sure he had it right, he repeated, "And the safe is behind a picture of President Kennedy."

"Correct."

Sheldon put the key and the paper in his pocket. "So I open the safe, remove a black bag, and come back here to the cab."

"With the bag," Vince prompted.

"With the bag." Why am I doing this, the dentist asked himself. "And you think there just might be two men hanging around in front of the building who should not see the bag?"

Vince nodded. "It's a possibility."

"What kind of guys?" the dentist asked nervously. "What are they . . ." He was almost embarrassed to say it but he wanted to know. ". . . after you or something?"

Vince laughed heartily and said with some appreciation, "You got some imagination, Shel. No, these are like competitors, y'know? And if they see that I have this black bag, I lose my competitive edge. That's all."

"Like Macy's and Gimbel's?"

"The perfect example, Shel," Vince nodded emphatically. "Really."

"Okay, let me get this over with." Sheldon got out of the cab.

Vince leaned out of the window and said, "Shelley?"

"Yeah?"

"I'll never forget this."

Listen, he's a little peculiar, Sheldon thought, but how much is he asking me to do? Abashed, he smiled at Vince and started down the street. A few steps later, the sight of Mo and Angie loitering in front of the old office building wiped the smile away. They were large and graphic, more three-dimensional than the thugs in the old Cagney movies. Sheldon sensed trouble. When he reached the building they had shifted their position, although Sheldon was sure it was unintentional—how could they know? They stood directly in his way.

Nervous and flustered, Sheldon took a step to the right. Simultaneously, obligingly, the two men stepped to their left, leaving the three of them right where they were, facing each other. Sheldon gave them a small smile, underplaying, nothing to call attention, just as far as his bicuspids. He stepped to the left as, anxious to cooperate, they stepped to their right.

"We'll stand still, okay?" one of the gorillas said.

"This happens all the time, doesn't it?" Sheldon said, trying to make it unimportant. He stepped around them mumbling, "Excuse me very much," and headed for the entrance to the building.

Mo and Angie watched the white-jacketed man, grateful for some distraction. They had been waiting all morning. "Making a house call, Doc?" Mo called.

Sheldon forced another smile and said, "That's right. One of those emergencies. You'll excuse me."

"Do your duty," Angie called.

Sheldon turned, as casual and nonchalant as possible, and walked into a glass door. Cursing under his breath, he rubbed his nose, found an open door, and walked through it.

Angie smiled at Mo, amused. "What a schmuck," he said, philosophically.

Crossing the small dim lobby, Sheldon, with shaking hand, took the key and the combination from his pocket. The key immediately slipped through his fingers and clattered to the floor. Stooping to retrieve it, Sheldon dropped the slip of paper with the combination to the safe. Grabbing for it, he somehow slid to all fours. He gathered both the objects, hoping the men outside had not noticed.

They had. Now, watching Sheldon cross the lobby and get into the self-service elevator, Mo said, "Nervous, wasn't he? Dropping everything."

"You think?" Angie asked, his tone indicating what he thought.

"Maybe," his companion answered, and as one they went into the building and watched the lights above the elevator ascend to number nine and stop.

"That's it," Mo said.

"Pretty cute. Using a doc." Angie pushed the elevator button.

Sheldon stepped off the elevator into a long and dingy corridor, the dust so heavy that it seemed to be pulling flakes of paint off the wall as he looked around. Most of the offices appeared to be empty, though a couple of typewriters somewhere clacked forlornly and one lonely voice yammered on a telephone.

Feeling as though his white jacket was absorbing the dirt from the atmosphere, Sheldon started down the corridor. What kind of offices can these be, he wondered. They can't be abortionists, that's legal now. Probably they're the addresses to which you send those coupons for the creams that delay your orgasms. At last he came to a door, half dirty frosted glass, with the words *Trans-Global Enterprises, Vincent J. Ricardo, President* lettered on it in flaking gilt. How trans, how global can any business in a building like this be, he wondered. Still shaking, he took the key from his pocket, dropped it again, retrieved it and opened the door.

The office was dark, a shade drawn down over the window. It looked, Sheldon decided, as though it had been furnished by the same decorator who designed the corridor. Probably Shmutz and Company, he thought. There was a grimy desk and two cracked, possibly leather chairs. He forded the dust to the window and tugged at the shade. With a crack like gunfire it rocketed up, exploded from its bracket, and fell, missing Sheldon's head by inches. In the pale light that seeped through the streaked window pane, Sheldon stared at the view: in the foreground a fire escape, in the distance, maybe four feet away, the wall of another building.

"Very nice," he mumbled aloud. "I send my daughter to Mount Holyoke so she can marry into this. Jesus Christ!"

He turned and surveyed the room. There was a world map Scotch-taped to one wall. It was studded with little red pins heavily concentrated in South and Central America. On the far wall, he saw the photo of President Kennedy. He moved toward the picture, taking the slip of paper from his pocket.

To Sheldon's surprise, there was an inscription on the picture. Squinting in the dim light, he leaned in close and read aloud, "To Vince. Well, at least we tried. Thanks for everything. Yours, John F. Kennedy. April 25th, 1961."

Of course, Vince could have written that himself. How would I know? But on the other hand, he reasoned, why would Vince think in April of 1961 that his son's future father-in-law would be looking at a picture of John F. Kennedy today? I wouldn't have thought so yesterday. He abandoned the whole thought-structure and pulled at the picture. It swung open on hinges, revealing a wall safe.

As Sheldon began to twirl the dial of the safe, down in the lobby Angie and Mo were getting into the elevator and pushing the button marked nine.

The cab stood empty in front of the Emerald Isle Bar and Grill on the corner of West Forty-sixth Street. Inside the bar, which was your basic bottom-of-the-line Irish saloon, the cabbie gulped a beer beside his passenger, who sipped some coffee. A half-dozen aging barflies were sprinkled around the dark room bathed in the flickering light of the TV screen, watching a game show.

"What is this show?" Vince asked, not allowing his perpetual search for information to be thwarted by the drama being enacted down the street.

The cabbie was amazed. "Are you kiddin', man? *The Price Is Right?* This is the all-American show."

"They gotta guess what all that crap is worth, that's the principle?" Vince grasped the idea at once.

"Right."

"Uh-huh," Vince nodded and asked the bartender, "Could I have some milk, please?" The bartender slid some milk across the bar and Vince said, "Thank you. Is this coffee freeze-dried, by the way?"

The bartender nodded, wondering what kind of nut this was.

"It's very good," Vince told him and turned to his companion. "This show been on the air long?"

"Since about 1911. I can't believe you never heard of *The Price Is Right.*"

"I don't get to watch that much television. I'm out of the country a lot."

"Really?" The cabbie set down his beer. "What do you do?"

"I work for the CIA," Vince told him, and turned his attention back to the TV set.

In the dark office with President Kennedy's face turned to the wall, Sheldon slid the knob on the safe around and pulled. Nothing happened. Nervously he checked the slip of paper in his hand again and mumbled, "Oh. Left. Damn," and started over. He was concentrating so hard he did not hear the elevator open in the grimy corridor. Nor did he hear the two gunmen tread softly in his direction.

"Three," Sheldon mumbled and tugged at the safe again. Nothing happened. Summoning extraction strength, he tugged harder and the safe door opened. The dentist stuck his hand into the black, yawning cavity.

On the other side of the office door, Angie and Mo stopped silently, the former touching the knob, moving it gingerly.

Up to his armpit in the safe, Sheldon froze, immobile, as though his entire body was Novocained. "Vince?" he whispered.

In the corridor Mo said softly, "He heard."

"Vince?" Sheldon whispered loud enough to be heard over the pounding of his heart.

In the corridor, Angie pulled out his gun and using the butt end, smashed the frosted glass of the door.

The shattered glass had not yet hit the floor when Sheldon screamed, and feverishly, automatically, pulled the black satchel out of the safe.

"Hold it!" he heard a voice call, low and intense, and saw a gun protruding through the hole in the glass. As he watched, another hand curled through the jagged opening and reached for the knob.

The disembodied voice spoke again. "Now, we don't mean you any harm whatsoever. This is strictly business, Doc. Just put the bag on the desk and step to the door."

The terrified dentist half-lurched to the desk. "I'm not the guy. He's my in-law," he said, supremely conscious that a pistol was pointed straight at him.

"Don't make any difference to me, Doc," the disembodied voice said. "Just put the bag down."

Sheldon nodded wordlessly, then from the depths of memory, back beyond his marriage, beyond dental school, to the draft and basic training, his body responded to the sight of the gun and he threw himself to the floor. He heard a shot ring out and the sound of the window behind him shattering. That's enough, he thought, I don't like people who play with guns. He jumped to his feet, raced to the window, threw it open, and, holding the black satchel, leaped onto the fire escape.

The office door burst open and Angie and Mo, calling, "Stop!" rushed in.

Sheldon was not about to obey orders. Mumbling-shrieking, "Oh God. GodGodGod!" he hurtled, stumbling, slipping, sliding down the rusty fire escape. He heard another shot ring out and echo either in his ears or in the airshaft. Pounding feverishly down the steps, not looking back, trying an appeal to their humanity if it existed, he called, "There's no reason to shoot me! I'm a dentist!"

The two men, guns drawn, peered out of the window. "Goddamn," Angie said. "I'll take the fire escape. You go down the stairs." Mo raced across the office and out the door as Angie climbed onto the fire escape and started after the fleeing dentist who was already four flights below. For a big man, he moved agilely, gaining on the frightened target almost at once.

Frantic, panting, his eyes seeking any escape, any protection from the man, the gun, the bullets, Sheldon charged along the fire escape. Passing a lit window, he glanced in and saw a bald businessman in boxer shorts being spanked by a bored black hooker. Startled, Sheldon stumbled and fell.

The hooker waved at him. "Ten dollars to watch, Jackson," she called. Sheldon scrambled to his feet and ran on.

This isn't real, he thought. It's a nightmare. A nightmare and soon I'm going to come out of the ether and Murray Weingart'll be standing in front of me holding my wisdom tooth and saying, "There, that was easy, wasn't it?" Somewhere above him, Angie, gun drawn, pounded down the steps, and deep in the bowels of the building his cohort, Mo, raced down the inky stairwell.

Sheldon had reached the bottom of the fire escape. He stared just for a terrified second at the ground, a long six feet away, and, hearing the footsteps from above, jumped. He landed heavily on his ass, feeling as though his backbone had catapulted up into his brainpan. Thinking, I really should join a gym, at least jog a little, he rose and, limping slightly, started running again.

Angie, a few flights above, displayed the form if not the physique of Bruce Jenner, jumping, spinning, racing toward the bottom of the fire escape.

Though he was not too interested in scenery, Sheldon realized that he was in a narrow alley between two buildings, between two brick walls that offered little protection if the mug above him opened fire. Hoping to present less of a target, he made a halfhearted effort at zigzagging and knocked over some garbage cans. For a second he feared the clatter might attract the gunman's attention, decided he was being silly and ran on.

Inside the building, Mo reached the bottom of the stairs and ran full tilt into a pair of double doors labeled *Fire Door—Emergency Only*. Pushing against them with all his considerable strength, he found them locked. Stopping a brief moment to collect his breath and wonder what the tenants would do in a fire, he pounded on them, yelling, "Hey! Emergency! Open the door!"

The denizens of Eighth Avenue, accustomed to the unaccustomed, showed little or no surprise at the sight of a sweaty dentist, his white jacket streaked with grime, clutching a black bag that might have contained the instruments of dentistry or a bomb from Puerto Rican nationalists, bursting from an alley and running down their street. Gasping and panting, Sheldon turned in what he hoped was the direction of the cab. He was a sedentary man, despite the fact he stood on his feet all day long, and he knew he could not take much more.

Back in the alley, Angie jumped catlike from the fire escape to the ground and, without losing a beat, ran on.

In the dank, sour-smelling quiet of the Emerald Isle Bar and Grill, Vince watched *The Price Is Right* with a consuming interest. "What a putz," he laughed at a contestant. "He guesses three hundred for that washer-dryer combination. Can you imagine?"

The cabbie, intrigued by more unusual events than price-guessing, stared at Vince. "I can't believe you work for the CIA," he said.

"Why not?"

"The cabbie laughed. "I don't know, man. I thought, you know, James Bond and all . . ." This funny little guy was no Sean Connery.

"Nah, they all look like me," Vince said. "I'm the classic Agency type . . . compact, muscular, low to the ground. Are you interested in joining? I'll tell you, the benefits are fantastic. The trick is not to get killed. That's really the key to the benefit program."

"You have to be pulling my leg," the driver said.

In the street, Sheldon's fright and exhaustion had combined into a blinding rage. "I'll kill him," he muttered under what breath he had left, as he raced on down the avenue.

Farther down the street behind him, Angie weaved around a startled passerby. As he ran, he pulled his gun into position and aimed at the fleeing figure a quarter of a block away.

The sharp report of the gun and the whoosh of the bullet speeding half a inch or so past his ear persuaded Sheldon he could still run. But just in case his newfound strength should fail, he looked to the sky for divine aid. "God," he prayed, "please don't let me die on West Forty-sixth Street!"

Lowering his gaze once more to the prosaic world he hoped to keep around him, Sheldon, through eyes awash with sweat, saw the haven of the cab, waiting at the corner to spirit him back to the safety of his office. With a final, Herculean spurt, he reached it, grabbing at the door. It was locked. Peering inside, he realized it was empty with the meter running. Fear and frustration welling up inside him, he began beating frantically on the hood, howling with deep emotion, "Vince, goddammit!"

It's interesting that grown people actually waste their time watching crap like this, Vince thought, as a contestant, only seven cents away from the right price, jumped up and down in an ecstasy of acquisition. The cabbie, hearing the sound of fist on metal and always concerned for the safety of his vehicle, looked through the window. He tapped his passenger.

"Hey, your friend is back," he said.

Vince turned and checked to see that it was indeed Sheldon pounding on the cab. "Okey-doke," he said calmly. He turned to the bartender and asked, "We square with you?"

The urban tom-tom beat of fist on taxi hood attracted more than the cab driver. Angie, coming into range, paused to fire again. Sheldon, clutching the black bag that was the cause of all his troubles, ducked behind the cab and sprawled in the gutter. Utterly bereft and miserable, feeling that the Higher Being had exhibited no interest in his plight whatsoever, he called the only other name he felt might help. "Vince! Vince!" he screamed into the traffic noise.

Angie reached the front of the Emerald Isle Bar and Grill and, gun drawn, advanced cautiously toward the parked cab. "For crying out loud," he called in some exasperation, the penalty for murder in broad daylight being what it was, "gimme the bag!" Hearing a sound behind him, he whirled with the expertise of a jungle fighter, but just a second too late.

Vince, already reaching for an inside pocket, had come out of the bar and, as the gunman turned, hit him with everything he had, which happened to be a gun butt. The burly gorilla fell to the sidewalk and Vince stepped delicately over him. "Shelley?" he called.

Sheldon, a victim of what was in a happier day called shell shock, crawled around the cab on all fours, apparently unable to speak.

"Shelley, you okay?" his concerned almost-in-law asked.

Behind Vince, the cabbie emerged from the bar and, looking up the street, called, "Hey! Watch it!" A split second later there was a gunshot.

Vince whirled from the quivering dentist and, almost as he turned, fired his pistol at the second gorilla running down the street, gun in hand. Mo stopped on a dime, his pistol flying from his hand, clutching his wrist in pain. Vince was suddenly aware that several policemen had come into his line of vision.

He turned to Sheldon and muttered, "Cops! C'mon. We really have to get out of here!" Then he helped the crumpled dentist to his feet and into the cab. The driver leaped in front and gunned the engine. Over the roar of the cab as it sped off up the block they could hear the wail of sirens.

Vince looked at Shelley with apology welling up and spilling over from his eyes. "Shelley," he said, softly, as though they were in church, "I'm really sorry that it turned out like that. I had no idea . . ."

Speeding crosstown in the cab, Sheldon understood his life had been spared and the only danger that hung over him now was of arrest. I could kill him, he thought, no matter how fast the cops go, I could kill him before they got here. Bug-eyed with fury, he yelled, "How could you?" and, lunging at Vince's throat, began to throttle him. All sense of in-law proprieties swept away in his rage, he cried, "I almost got killed!"

Hanging onto the madman's throat in the swaying, speeding cab, Shelley was too intent on murder to hear Vince's strangulated "I didn't—"

"You have dinner in my house, then you drag me out of my office and set me up to get killed!"

Vince shook his head, attempting to speak, his voice growing fainter as his windpipe contracted between the hands of molar-pulling strength. "I'd really like to explain . . ." he wheezed.

"No explaining!" the enraged dentist cried. But seeing that the face was turning blue, recalling the penalty for murder, no matter how justified, he let go of the man's throat, bouncing him in the same gesture off the seat. "Just get out of my life!"

"I completely understand," Vince gasped.

"You don't understand! How could you understand? You're crazy! I understand. I understand you're a freakin' lunatic!"

"I know your appointment was for nine-thirty, Mrs. Fineshreiber," Evita said again.

"It's just a tooth. One tooth broke off my bridge," the dumpy, middle-aged lady said, one hand covering her mouth. "I was eating a piece of bread . . ." To make her accusation of Dr. Kornpett's incompetence even stronger, she added, "A soft piece of bread."

"Doctor had to step out for a minute," Evita said. She was considering switching into Spanish as a last line of defense if the woman continued to nag her.

"A minute!" Mrs. Fineshreiber shrieked, dropping her hand from her mouth in amazement at the barefaced lie. "I been here since nine twenty-five, a dentist I haven't seen."

"I'm very sorry, Mrs. Fineshreiber. It was an emergency," Evita lied, raising her voice as she heard angry mumbles from the rest of the crowd. It was hot in the waiting room and the steam rising from the furious patients was beginning to fog her glasses. And *Madre de Dios,* Evita was upset enough to think in her native tongue, where was he?

"I have to go to a B'nai B'rith luncheon," Mrs. Fineshreiber yelled, but the hand over her mouth deadened the sound somewhat.

"You'll make it," Evita snapped. "It's only ten-thirty."

"It's in Brooklyn," Mrs. Fineshreiber snarled. "I'm the entertainment chairman and I don't have a front tooth."

"I was nine-fifteen," a pregnant woman announced from the sofa across the room. Just then the door opened. Every anxious head in the room turned in its direction and saw Dr. Kornpett. He looked, Evita thought, as though he'd been dragged down Madison Avenue by a leaky garbage truck.

The dentist shoved the door closed behind him, but before it could slam, it bounced back and the man whose son was marrying Dr. Kornpett's wonderful daughter followed him in. He was carrying a little black bag.

"I completely sympathize with your feelings," the husky little man said urgently.

"Then go! Leave me alone already!" the dentist screamed. Mrs. Fineshreiber, shocked, steadied herself against Evita's desk, the pregnant woman cried, "Oh!" and two patients dropped their *National Geographics*.

Sheldon was suddenly aware of the roomful of patients staring at him. Mortified, he turned his back on the room and, lowering his voice, whispered as forcefully as he knew how, "Please! Go away!"

"I really want to oblige you, Shel," Vince said, "but I've got a conscience. I can't leave things where they are. I feel terrible." He too, became aware of his audience and smiled at them charmingly. "His wonderful daughter is marrying my son, Tommy."

There were a few approving "oohs" and "ahhs" and murmurs of "Congratulations" from the waiting room, but the pregnant woman said, "I was nine-fifteen," and Mrs. Fineshreiber announced, "I have a luncheon in Sheepshead Bay."

"Thank you very much," Dr. Kornpett said with as much dignity as he could muster. "Sorry I'm late. We'll try and speed things along." He moved rapidly across the

72

room toward the dental chamber. Like a faithful hound, Vince followed him. At the door, Sheldon stopped, turned and whispered fiercely, "Go!"

"I can't. It's too important."

From the dental chair where she sat, mouth open, still unmoving, Mrs. Adelman had heard the commotion in the outer office. Hoping it might mean release from her uncomfortable position and a chance to scratch her back, which had been itching for what seemed like hours, she rolled her eyes in the direction of the door. She heard it open, and Dr. Kornpett came into her line of vision.

"Oh God!" he said. "Mrs. Adelman, you kept still the entire time?" She nodded. "Jesus, I'm really sorry," he said, wondering if this could in some way leave him open for a malpractice suit. "Please, you can close your mouth now. Bite down."

At last, Mrs. Adelman sighed mentally, but when she tried to close her mouth, it wouldn't move. It was as though from long disuse, the jaws had frozen. Oh my God, she thought, I'll never be able to bite down again. How will I eat? No steak, no licorice, no solids at all. A life of chicken soup. The dentist, understanding, a flicker of fear in his eyes, was putting one hand under her chin, the other on top of her head, pushing, trying vainly to help her close. At least, she thought, it's frozen open. They won't have to feed me intravenously.

She heard the noise of someone else entering the room behind her and a man's voice saying, "Shelley?"

The dentist whirled toward the sound and cried, "Our relationship is over! I can't do anything about the marriage, but with us, it's finished."

The chunky man she'd seen before whose son was marrying Dr. Kornpett's lovely daughter came into view carrying a black bag and shaking his head regretfully. "Were that only true," he said.

"What the hell are you talking about?" the dentist screamed. Mrs. Adelman tried to make some sound, but it was too late, she'd missed her chance. The other man was opening the black bag and showing its contents to the dentist.

"What are they?" Kornpett asked, peering into the bag.

"I'm so embarrassed," the other man said.

"What are they?" the dentist repeated, louder, angrier.

The other man looked the dentist in the eye. "Shel, you've just been running down Forty-sixth Street with a billion dollars worth of engravings stolen from the United States Mint. Within twenty-four hours the FBI, the Treasury Department, and the World Bank is gonna be all over the both of us, unless of course the mob gets to us first, which is a very good possibility. Shel, we're in big trouble, but if I play my cards right . . ."

Mrs. Adelman had been watching the dentist, saw his complexion go from ruddy anger to the dead white of fear. She was, however, unprepared for him to faint, and anyway, having sat still for all this time, she couldn't move. He must've weighed one hundred and seventy pounds and it all came crashing down on her. How can I tell the doctor how many ribs are broken when I can't close my mouth? she wondered.

Despite all, the dark man finished his thought. ". . . we could come out all right." Then he put his arms around the dentist and lifted him off Mrs. Adelman. Holding the dentist upright, the man looked back at the patient, staring into her mouth. Then he looked into her eyes and said, "You can rinse now, dear."

7

Why do I always pick the longest line in the bank? Carol asked herself. She had already switched twice. Once to a short line which proved to have an elderly lady with a foreign money order and a total inability to deal with the information she was given. Then back to the first line, three people behind her original place. One of those three then drew a locked leather envelope from her purse and proceeded to hold up the line with a deposit that looked like four hundred checks, probably the year's take from some mail-order firm.

At long last Carol advanced to the teller's window and managed to smile at the girl framed in it. "Hi," she said.

"Hello, Mrs. Kornpett. All set for the wedding?"

I don't have time to chat, Carol thought. She said,

"We're getting there," politely, hoping to call a halt to conversation.

"How's Barbara? She nervous?" the teller went on.

Shoeless, Carol thought. "She doesn't show it but I'm sure she is. My husband is the jumpiest of us all right now," Carol answered, not realizing how close to the truth she was.

But the teller wasn't through. Relentlessly, she went on. "Isn't that always the case? There's just some things men don't handle as well as we do."

Female chauvinist pig, Carol decided. "I suppose so," she said, hoping the teller was finished chatting at last.

"Now what can we do for you today? Cash a check, I bet?"

Finally, Carol thought. "Not really. I found something . . ." She opened her purse and removed the engraving. "Believe it or not, I found this in my cellar this morning and I just don't know what to make of it, or do with it . . ." She slid it across the counter to the teller, who picked it up.

"Heavy, isn't it?" the girl said. She looked at it more closely. "My goodness. This is some kind of engraving."

"For a five hundred."

The teller squinted winsomely at the engraving. "I think you're right," she said. "You found this in your cellar, Mrs. Kornpett, is that what you said?"

"This morning." And it's rapidly becoming late afternoon, Carol added mentally.

The teller laughed. "Geez, I never have that kind of luck."

"Do you have any idea of . . . what I should do with it or what it's worth?"

"Gee, I really don't know, Mrs. Kornpett. I've never even seen one of these! You know, I could ask our branch manager. Do you mind waiting?"

No more than I minded childbirth, Carol thought, but answered, "No," resignedly. "I'd really like to resolve this somehow."

"Sure, I don't blame you. Let me ask him," the teller said. Then she walked away.

Carol leaned against the counter, convinced that with her luck it would be a long wait.

Across the floor of the small suburban bank, Barbara, wearing jeans and T-shirt and carrying a small shopping bag, pushed open the door and came in. Glancing around quickly, she saw her mother and walked past the line to her.

"Ready?" she asked.

"In a second. Did you get the shoes?"

"No, they were all awful." Barbara made a face. "I got a pair of tennis sneakers so it wouldn't be a total loss."

"You've got to get shoes."

"I know, I know," Barbara singsonged. "Tomorrow I'll go into the city and try Bloomingdale's and I. Miller and Bendel. Worse comes to worse, I'll wear my clogs on Sunday."

Feeling her temper going and deciding she deserved a little fit, Carol snapped, "You're not going to wear clogs at your wedding."

"Nobody'll see them," Barbara said with irritating reasonableness.

The teller, by now, had attracted the bank manager's attention and was standing by his desk. The portly gentleman was seated, staring at the engraving with a concern as obvious as his toupee. "My God," he said.

"What?" the teller asked. Wordlessly, the man pointed to a newspaper on his desk, edging it over a little so the teller could see a headline: *U.S. Mint truck robbed. Millions in engravings taken. Sixth in a series of international heists.* Feeling a little woozy, the teller grabbed the edge of the desk. "I might faint," she announced.

The bank manager ignored her. He took a sheet of paper from his desk and scanned it. "We got a memo this morning," he said, "concerning counterfeits that might be printed off these plates."

"But they wouldn't really be counterfeit," the teller pointed out.

"That's the problem; they just have to take those serial numbers out of circulation."

"Are the serial numbers—" The teller was unable to finish the question. There was a strange tingling in her ankles. It was the most exciting experience she had had since she came in second for Homecoming Queen.

The branch manager opened the top drawer of his desk, took out a magnifying glass, and, with some sense of the occasion, gravely studied the engraving and compared the numbers on it with the sheet of paper. "Oh boy," he said and nodded, "We got one."

Barbara considered telling Carol she would prefer to be married barefoot. The way her mother was ranting on about the shoes, she was giving them far more time than she had given the Facts of Life. Hopeless. "Let's not fight about it," Barbara said, taking the easy way out. "I'll go to the city tomorrow and probably find an acceptable pair of shoes."

But once launched, Carol's argument continued under its own power. "Clogs are out of the question."

"Will you stop?" Barbara asked harshly. Then she heard a voice say, "Mrs. Kornpett?"

Carol, mouth open to reply to Barbara, turned and was a little startled to see the bank manager standing beside her. The teller was there, too, but she had stopped smiling. What made it all rather sinister for Carol were the pair of security guards bookended around the other two.

"Yes?" Carol gulped.

"Would you mind stepping over to my office for a moment? I'd like to ask you a few questions," the bank manager said.

Maybe shoes are not the most important thing in life, Carol thought.

With shaking hands, Sheldon had raced through his morning appointments in triple time. Like a speeded up dentist in a Chaplin comedy, he had scraped, drilled, mixed, filled, fitted, cajoled, and sympathized. Frantically nervous, he was aware that the FBI, the CIA, the Treasury Department, and God knew who else might be on his tail. And meanwhile, Vince Ricardo was on his back. The little man demanded to talk with him, to "clear up the situation," as he said. Though Sheldon reminded him of the crowded office, the patients, the man absolutely refused to leave his office. Vince said he would wait till Shelley was less busy, but he would not even wait in the waiting room, which Sheldon had pointed out was designed for that purpose. Instead, Vince sat in the corner of the office, the black bag clutched securely in his lap, and excercised his inquiring mind with lucid, pointed questions concerning Sheldon's methods and techniques.

"Why do you use the corkscrew thing for root-canal work instead of the big drill?"

"If it's really a canal, what does it connect?"

"Is a gold filling really better than a silver filling, considering the price of gold on the international market?"

And when Sheldon broke the drill head on Mr. d'Angelo's canine, Ricardo asked, "How about plastic?"

By eleven forty-five, still shaking and wet with perspiration, Sheldon had cleared the waiting room. With fifteen minutes open until his next patient, he turned to Vince and said, "Now . . ."

"Y'know, it's fascinating work you do, Shel," the man said, nodding as he spoke. "Fascinating."

"Thanks, but—"

"It's remarkable to me how they got all these doctor shows on the television, y'know, and there's never been one dentist show."

"Right," Sheldon said and opened his mouth to return to the main question in his mind.

"It could be terrific . . . like, Robert Young as a kindly dentist, each week solving some major problem—a girl who can't get a guy cause o' this overbite . . . a middle-aged man, such as ourselves, whose family life is being destroyed because his gums are receding . . ."

"Ricardo," Sheldon snarled, then softened it to "Vince," not wanting to antagonize the man, wanting only to get him out of his office and his life, "you have not sat here for an hour and a half to discuss television."

"You're right, Shelley, you're absolutely right. I think we should talk."

"We have nothing more to talk about," the dentist said

through clenched teeth, hoping he was right. Ricardo looked at him quizzically and patted the little black bag. "Talk," Sheldon said, resigned.

"Not here."

"Why not? Do you think they've bugged my drill?" Sheldon howled.

"We could get interrupted and I really want you to understand what's going on."

"You're not going to take me someplace and have me steal something else?" Sheldon asked.

"No. I swear, Shelley, that part of the operation is over. I just thought we could maybe have a bite of lunch."

Sheldon closed his eyes, nodded, opened his eyes, and checked his watch. "Ten minutes," he said. "Ten minutes. At twelve o'clock I'm adjusting a chaise bridge."

"Terrific," Vince said. "That'll be plenty of time." He started for the door, then, stopping next to the dentist's workshelf, he placed the black bag on it. "I'll just leave this here."

"No!" Sheldon screamed. "Get that out of here!"

"Shelley," Vince said reasonably, "would you want to carry a billion dollars worth of stolen engravings into a restaurant? Suppose you're crossing the street and you're hit by a bus and some cop picks them up. There could be a lot of questions."

For a brief moment the dentist considered throwing himself under a bus, and had almost persuaded himself it was not a bad idea when he thought of the wedding on Sunday and how disappointed Barbara would be. "All right," he said. "But you'll come back and get them?"

"If that's what you want, Shelley, sure," Ricardo assured him.

Then how will I get you out, Sheldon wondered as Vince continued, "Is there an Italian restaurant in this neighborhood? I could sure go for some canneloni." He opened the door.

Shelley pointed at the black bag. "You're going to leave that there? Out in the open?" he demanded. Vince shrugged. Sheldon grabbed the bag and looked wildly around the office for some place to hide it. Seeing the wastebasket that was used for the dirty dental bibs, he raced to it, opened it, and with one hand held up a bunch of the bloodied paper bibs and with the other jammed the bag into the receptacle. He dumped the crumpled papers back, ruffled them up slightly to hide the bag, closed the basket, and stood up.

"When does the garbage man come?" Vince asked practically.

"After six."

"Okay," Vince said and left the office.

As the elevator door closed on them, Sheldon saw the chaise bridge he was to adjust and the man around it step out of the elevator on the opposite side of the hall, and nervously checked his watch. It was already one minute to twelve.

He hurried Vince down Madison Avenue to the nearest coffee shop, installed them in a booth, and ordered some soup, the only food he felt his nervous stomach could contend with.

They sat in silence till the waitress dumped their food before them, largely because Sheldon could not think where to begin his questioning, and Ricardo, for once, did not seem anxious to talk.

Sheldon, still pale, still shaking somewhere deep inside, picked up his spoon and forced some soup into his mouth.

"You feel a little better?" Vince asked solicitously.

Sheldon nodded.

"You were very smart to get that split-pea soup," Vince said. "It looks delicious. May I?" He waved his spoon in the direction of Sheldon's bowl.

Soup, Sheldon thought. The world is in flames and he's complimenting me on my soup. Wearily he nodded and the chunky man dipped his spoon in Sheldon's bowl, balanced it carefully across the table, and sipped it judiciously as if it were a fine wine.

"Mmm," Vince mm'd. "Very nice. A little greasy but very nice. You should crumble up some Saltines into it; that absorbs the grease."

Sheldon stared unseeing off into the middle distance. Thank you, Julia Child, he thought, or thank you, Amy Vanderbilt, or better yet, thank you, God, for allowing me to sit in this awful place eating greasy pea soup that doesn't have Saltines in it, which is preferable to eating it in jail. Or being dead, he thought, remembering the sound of the bullet whistling past his ear on Eighth Avenue. He shivered. I'm delaying, he thought. I'm not facing the facts. The X rays have been developed, it's time I read them. He looked at Vince across the table and spoke.

"Those engravings, they're real?"

"Oh, yeah, they're real all right."

"Where did you get them?"

"Look, this may sound a little peculiar," Vince began.

"I know it will sound peculiar," Sheldon stopped him. "Where did you get them?"

"I stole them."

"From whom?"

"The U.S. Mint," Vince said as though it was the most natural thing in the world. "I mean, where else could you steal engravings for currency?"

Sheldon's head spun around the room to see if anyone had heard. Vince had not lowered his voice, and a small, crowded coffee shop in midtown Manhattan was no place to hold an essentially intimate conversation like this. Especially at lunch time. Especially with Vince. He is not the kind of person to hold any kind of confidential conversation with, Sheldon thought, even in the barren wastes of Siberia.

"Y'see, I told the Agency . . ." the man's voice blared on.

"What agency?" Sheldon whispered, leaning in across the table.

"What agency?" Vince asked the world, showing them the idiocy of Sheldon's question. "The CIA."

"What have they got to do with it?" the dentist asked, a chill wave surfing down his back.

"I work for them," Vince announced. "I work for the CIA. That was why I stole the engravings from the mint. Oh, not alone. I had some help," he admitted modestly. He sat opposite Sheldon in a booth that was open to a hundred pairs of ears, telling his story gallantly, bravely and at a decibel count the Bee Gees would have admired. It was as though he felt he had nothing to hide; the book of his life was open no matter how many top secrets were printed in its pages. He was a husky Italian Joan of Arc munching a sandwich.

Sheldon counted five to allow the informational filling to set in the cavity of his mind, then articulated carefully, "I'm really trying to get this straight. You robbed the U.S. Mint for the CIA? Is that accurate?"

"Completely." Vince seemed pleased at Sheldon's grasp of the situation.

"And because of who?"

"Let me just put this in a nutshell. I mean, there's various nuances and shadings, but let's skip over them for now, okay?"

Sheldon said, "Fine," but was convinced the man was fudging the issue, conning him. Again.

"Okay." Vince took off. "Over the past six months there's been a succession of major heists, all pulled off the same way. First the English mint, then the German mint, then the Swiss mint. Bing, bing, bing." The bing, bing, bing, reminded Sheldon of gunfire and it made him uneasy. "We . . . the agency . . ." his companion was continuing.

"The CIA," Sheldon said, determined to get it straight, point by point, no matter how many bowls of soup it took.

"That's right. The Agency knows these engravings are going down to Latin America as part of a plot to totally destroy the U.S. economy."

Aha, Sheldon thought. We're back to Latin America. "Does this have anything to do with tsetse flies?" he asked.

"Shel, I'm very serious." Vince looked very serious. "You gotta understand that these little banana countries down there owe billions and billions of dollars to the West. And since they ain't got a pot to piss in, there's no way they can ever pay back. No way...unless suddenly there's such an unbelievable inflation that paper money ain't worth wiping your butt on. Once they get these plates in the bag, they're set."

"Set for what?"

Vince leaned forward and spoke even more urgently. "Shel, what do you think's going to happen if they start running off this dough and suddenly there's trillions of extra dollars and francs and marks floating around? You get a collapse of confidence in the currency, gold riots, arson, looting, political chaos, atonal music, expressionism. Like Germany before Hitler. I mean, what do you think people are going to do when a six-pack of Budweiser costs twelve hundred bucks?"

Sheldon stared at the man. Alice, he decided. He isn't Joan of Arc, he's Alice living in his own wonderland, robbing the rich to keep the poor from robbing the rich, and, realizing he had promoted Vince from Alice to an out-of-focus Robin Hood, he nodded and said, "That would be awful," just to say something.

"You think I'm bullshitting, right?" Vince said, cutting to the heart of the matter.

Sheldon said, "No, not at all," but even he didn't think it sounded convincing.

"Well, they thought I was bullshitting," Vince said.

"Who?

"The Agency. I told them that the thing to do was rob the U.S. Mint, really rob it ... professionally ... then take the engravings to Latin America and find out where the action was." Vince's face fell slightly, a hint of disillusionment with his employers coming into his voice. "But they thought it was too risky."

Sheldon's stomach, temporarily lulled, turned over, revved up, and proceeded churning double time. He leaned into the table. "Wait a minute." I must get this straight, he told himself. "The CIA turned this down? I thought you were doing it for them?"

"I am."

"So they're behind it?"

"No. I did this on my own."

Sheldon spilled the soup over his hands.

"You okay?" Vince asked, solicitously, as though he realized that a dentist with scalded hands was an unemployed dentist.

"You robbed the United States Mint on your own?" Sheldon's voice rose dangerously, and several heads left their troughs in the crowded coffee shop and stared. Vince didn't seem to mind. Still unable to control the pitch of his voice, Sheldon blared out, "The CIA thought it was too crazy—"

"Too risky," Vince corrected.

"So you just went ahead and did it on your own. With those gangsters. My God!"

"I couldn't do it by myself, Shel," Vince explained sensibly. "I had to hire people, and I must say, they've turned out to be quite a disappointment, wanting their money right away, trying to harm you . . ." The look in Vince's eyes said there positively wasn't any Santa Claus.

Sheldon held up his hand. "Wait a minute, I want to get this straight. The CIA didn't authorize this, you hired gangsters." Suddenly aware of his audience, he managed to lower his voice. "So you committed a crime, right?"

"Of course." Vince's tone made the question redundant.

"It's a Federal rap." Then carefully, as to a child, he explained, "That's why the FBI is after us."

"Stop the 'us' already! Just listen for a minute. If you get caught, will the CIA come out and say, 'He works for us. It's okay'?"

"No."

"No?" The dentist's big brown eyes became so glassy it was as though he'd put in contact lenses when no one was looking.

"No," Vince said. "I'm out in the cold on this. If I bring it off, I'm a hero in the Agency. If I get caught, the Agency will shred my records and say they never heard of me. I'll be in the slammer for twenty-five years. Minimum."

"But not me," Sheldon said quickly. "It's just you. I mean, I empathize, but I'm not involved in this in any way now, right?"

Vince nodded vigorously, encouragingly. "That's virtually true," he said.

"What virtually?" Sheldon's voice skidded up again, his stomach an outboard motor in his jockey shorts. "I did you a favor. I got the bag. I almost got killed. It's finished."

"That's right," Vince agreed. "You're free and clear. As soon as we get that engraving out of your house."

"What engraving?" I'm going insane, Sheldon thought. I woke up this morning, ate my oatmeal, I was sane. Now I'm insane.

"An engraving," Vince answered.

"From the bag?"

"That's right. I thoughtlessly left one in your basement last night."

Sheldon had already questioned his sanity; this time he questioned his hearing. He could not believe his ears. "In my basement?" he shouted.

"Why are you getting so excited?" Vince asked.

"Why am I getting excited?" Sheldon screamed, and a few heads turned toward their table. "The central piece of evidence in the biggest Federal crime since the atomic spy case is sitting in my basement in Teaneck . . ." He had the full attention of the coffee shop now, customers, waitresses. Even the short-order cook, his spatula poised over a burning western omelet, was staring. "And you ask me why I might be getting excited!"

Now it was Vince's turn to become angry. He whirled in the booth, his eyes flashing at the startled faces that crowded the coffee shop. "Go back to your lunches," he called. "Do I meddle in your business?"

Furtively, with the tacit New York pretense that the catastrophe had never happened, and if it had happened, they were looking the other way at the time, the patrons returned to their meals. Vince looked back to Sheldon. "Shelley . . ." he said, placatingly.

"If I didn't love my daughter so much, I think I'd call the cops."

"Shelley, I understand your concern, but, believe me, I've been with the Agency for twenty-five years. This thing is basically going like clockwork."

"Clockwork. I want that thing out of my house." Sheldon's voice was now dangerously, threateningly low.

Vince looked at his watch. "In two hours, a man calling himself Smith will arrive at your house to read your gas meter. Actually, he's gonna pick up the engraving."

"In two hours," Sheldon repeated.

"At the latest." Vince waved at the waitress. "I gotta run," he told Sheldon and called, "Check," to the girl. "I'll pick this up, Shel," he announced.

"Vince, I want you to understand something. If that . . ." Sheldon couldn't bring himself to name the object that could buy untold material things or, conversely, twenty-five years in the slammer . . . "thing," he decided to call it, "is not removed from my house in two hours, so help me God, I'm going to call off the wedding. I will not allow my family to be jeopardized—"

"Shel, I understand," Vince protested. "I'd do the same thing if I were you." The waitress dropped the check on the table. Vince took it and rose, heading for the cashier.

"I'm not kidding," his guest said following him.

Vince threw a ten on the cashier's desk. "I believe you," he said. "But take it from me, it will be done and we'll look back at this episode in the years to come—around the Christmas tree—and we'll have a good laugh about it." He clapped the unconvinced Sheldon on his back. "Take care," he said, and turning, sped through the revolving door of the shop.

In an instant reflex, Sheldon dashed after him. "Vince!" he cried. The man was already at the curb, hailing a cab.

As the cab drove up, Vince turned. "Shelley?" he said, as though he were surprised to see him.

"What about that thing in my office?" For a moment Vince stared blankly at the dentist. "The black bag?" Sheldon enunciated firmly.

"Oh, yeah," Vince said and opened the cab door. "You take it home, I'll have Tommy pick it up later."

"No!" Sheldon cried.

"It's just a little black bag, Shelley," Vince said reasonably. "Nobody connects the contents with you. What time you get home?"

"Seven," Sheldon answered automatically, knowing he was being sucked further down the vortex.

"He'll be there. It'll all be over at seven o'clock. I promise you." Vince waved and stepped into the cab.

Sheldon grabbed the door before the man could close it. There was one more thing he simply had to understand. "Vince," he said.

"What?"

"What's that picture of Kennedy in your office? 'At least we tried,' " Sheldon quoted. "What did that mean?"

"That referred to the Bay of Pigs expedition."

Sheldon was astounded. It was difficult to believe. Yet he'd seen the picture with his own eyes. "You were involved in the Bay of Pigs?" he asked.

"Involved?" Vince smiled. "It was my idea. See you tomorrow, Shel."

"I am definitely canceling my account," Carol said as she braked for a red light.

"Mother," Barbara began placatingly.

"Fifteen years! I've had an account there fifteen years and they treated me like a criminal."

"They were just doing their job."

"Their job?" Carol shrieked, and the car lurched forward in comparable agitation as the light turned green. "All those questions? I could have just forgotten that silly old engraving. I don't know what is is. I don't know how it got there! I'm having a wedding Sunday. My back lawn has been ruined with that tent . . . Do you know how much I've spent on the Lawn Doctor to get that grass to grow?

I still need a half-slip, you need shoes, and I haven't got your father's suit back from the cleaner's, and they spend hours questioning me like I was the Brinks gang!"

She turned the car into their street. "I will speak to your father tonight, and tomorrow I'm definitely canceling the account."

"Don't they hold your mortgage?" Barbara asked.

"I'll cancel that, too." Carol pulled into the driveway and asked, "What's that?" There was a panel truck parked at the curb in front of their house.

"Rubin's Catering?" Barbara suggested.

"They were here this morning." Carol got out of the car and fished in her purse for the keys. A man got out of the panel truck and walked up the driveway toward them. "Now what?" Carol mumbled.

"Do you want something?" Barbara called to the man. Carol thought there was something sinister about the man. He was wearing a shirt and tie. He stopped in front of her.

"I've come to read your gas meter," the man said.

"My gas meter?" Carol repeated, and the man nodded, a strange expression in his eyes, as though he was telling her something more than that he planned to read the gas meter. "My house," Carol said very carefully, "runs entirely on electricity."

The man thought for a moment. "My name is Smith," he said.

Wondering which of the neighbors would be in if she had to run for it, Carol said, "My name is Kornpett. My house is electrified. No gas."

The man considered the problem. Finally, he spoke. "I've come to read the electric meter," he said.

"The electric meter," Carol said, stalling for time. Barbara walked around the car to her mother.

"In the basement," Mr. Smith said, nodding meaningfully.

"It's been read," Carol said, her voice rising slightly.

"My name is Smith," he repeated, louder.

"What's your first name?" Carol asked, feeling idiotic but also thinking she'd be safe as long as she kept him talking.

"John," the man answered after a moment's hesitation.

"Get his license number, Barbara," Carol said pointedly.

"Yes," her daughter said and inched even closer to Carol, her eyes not leaving the man's face.

"Please. It'll only take a minute. In the basement," the man said.

"My daughter's got your number, Mr. John Smith. If you don't get out of here right now, I am going to call the police," Carol said, trying to remember whether it was "Fire!" or "Rape!" you were supposed to yell to attract people's attention. The entire day, even without the wedding, would have been too much for her.

Mr. Smith was staring at her, his mouth moving as though he was trying to phrase some difficult thought. The two women stared back. It was a moment inexplicably caught out of time and place. There seemed to be nothing in the world at that moment to Carol but the man's face with its tortured, questioning expression and the suspicious collar and tie.

"Go 'way," Barbara said with a certain frantic authority. She hefted the shoe bag with the sneakers in it as though it were a weapon.

Surprisingly, Mr. Smith began to back away across the front lawn, and Carol was engulfed with a feeling of pride and gratitude to Barbara; brave, sensible, pragmatic, a helluva kid. As she watched Smith move back slowly, she became aware of the sound of a car rolling into her driveway. Carol glanced quickly over her shoulder and saw not one, but two huge black cars with some kind of insignia on their doors coming to a stop on either side of her Toyota. She looked back at Smith, who was moving faster, and realized it was not Barbara's brave gesture with the shoe bag but the arrival of the strangers that had frightened him off.

She heard car doors opening and turned back in the direction of the black cars. Several men were getting out, a tall blond man advancing on her. What now, she wondered, I can't take much more.

"Mrs. Kornpett?" the blond man asked, coming closer. There were six or eight men behind him now. Peripherally she saw Smith getting into the panel truck. Maybe she was better off with him. He was only one. Idiotically, she considered calling him back to read whatever meter he wished.

"She's Mrs. Kornpett," Carol heard Barbara say, cool, controlled. Well, she's young, Carol thought, and *her* daughter isn't getting married Sunday.

"My name is Thornton," the man said, flashing some sort of identification. "I'm with the Treasury Department."

For a moment her house whirled around Carol and the sun seemed to drop from the New Jersey sky. She understood she was on the verge of fainting. The roar of an engine brought her back to her senses and the house settled back on its foundation. She saw that Thornton was looking to the street, and her eye followed his gaze. The panel truck was driving off.

"Who was that?" the man from the Treasury Department asked, and Carol knew she was completely unable to answer.

"He came to read the gas meter," she heard Barbara say, and congratulated herself again on the wonderful cool-in-a-crisis child she had raised.

"I'd like to ask you a few questions, Mrs. Kornpett. May we go inside?"

"Of course." It was Barbara to the rescue again. "Come on, Mother," she said, and she took the keys from Carol's hand, grasped her arm, and led her to the front door.

Touched and grateful, Carol watched Barbara fumble the key into the lock. As her daughter opened the door and Carol went in, she managed to whisper, "If you really want them, you can get the plastic shoes."

8

The three cars were still parked in the driveway of the colonial house on the quiet street in Teaneck. In the soft, hazy, six-thirty light of the June night, Carol's little Toyota looked dwarfed, almost surrounded, as indeed it was, by the two large black cars bearing the insignia of the United States Treasury Department. It was as if the two official vehicles had not actually handcuffed the little Japanese but were expecting trouble and were determined to block off all escape routes.

In the attractively furnished living room, Barbara, looking at her mother and half a dozen T-men, felt the way the Toyota looked. Not exactly captured but certainly not free to go.

"This is absurd," she told the room. "I feel like Bonnie and Clyde."

Thornton, the principal T-man, looked at her. "I wish it was absurd, Miss Kornpett. But it's a very serious matter."

One of his aides came in from the kitchen and announced, "Nothing else in the basement." Barbara wished she could get over the feeling that these men looked like the slightly over-age chorus in a Broadway musical. Maybe *How to Succeed in Law Enforcement Without Really Trying.*

"How long has your husband practiced dentistry, Mrs. Kornpett?" a third T-man asked.

"He's had his own practice since nineteen—" Carol hesitated, trying to remember, accomplishing it by taking Barbara's age and subtracting. "Sixty," she finished. She was calmer now, almost accustomed after two hours to having a phalanx of T-men in her house. Idly she wondered if she should serve coffee, or, since it was six-thirty, should it be drinks?

"Always in New York?" a fourth man asked. They split up their lines like a chorus, Barbara noticed.

"That's right," Carol said. "He shared a practice with Dr. Murray Weingart in Brooklyn for a couple of years, then opened his own practice in Manhattan."

"He was sergeant-at-arms of the Long Island Dentists Guild," Barbara threw in.

"He's always kept regular hours?" Thornton asked.

"He comes through that door at seven o'clock every single night," her mother answered.

"Any tax trouble?" the third T-man asked, and Barbara almost told him he'd jumped the second man's turn.

"None. He overpays," Carol said firmly, as though it was a frequent subject for argument in the colonial house. "His accountant tells him to take all these deductions but he refuses." She decided definitely against serving. Let's keep this strictly business, she thought, and asked for the third or fourth time, "Please, tell me what this is all about. What's with the engraving?"

"That's what we'd like to know, Mrs. Kornpett," Thornton answered. "But I'm sure that if everything you have told us is accurate, that there's a very simple explanation."

"This is so insane," Barbara could not refrain from saying. "When you meet my father . . . I mean, he is the least likely person to be mixed up in anything."

The third man smiled. "I'm sure he is, miss."

The Least Likely Person to Be Mixed Up in Anything pulled his late-model BMW into the exit ramp and rolled off Route 4. Tired, but fairly relaxed, the Least Likely Person hummed along with the Ray Coniff Singers, who were crooning the Beatles' "Michelle" on the easy-listening station to which the radio was tuned. There was a black satchel containing stolen engravings worth billions on the seat beside the Least Likely Person to Be Mixed Up in Anything.

"*Ma belle* . . ." he hummed. ". . . say these words so you'll understand . . ."

Lazily, in the rhythm of the song, the car wound through the quiet, immaculate streets of the familiar neighborhood. I could practically turn the ignition key and let the car take me, Sheldon thought idly. Not really meaning that, he turned the wheel himself and the car came around into his block.

"Say these words . . ." Sheldon sang, and thought, almost seven. He looked at the black bag beside him. In ten minutes Tommy will pick it up and everything will be as it was. My biggest problem will be getting through the wedding. Then suddenly he wondered, Do I want my daughter marrying a man who's an accessory after the fact in the biggest heist of the decade? But, he thought further, I'm an accessory, too. At that moment, he caught sight of his driveway and his accessory's heart almost stopped beating. Two black cars . . . the Treasury Department insignia burned into his retina. He slammed on his brakes, tore his eyes away from the unfamiliar cars to see two strange men, who had obviously come in them, standing in his own familiar window.

"Holy shit!" he said.

As the sound of Sheldon's brakes, squealing in rebellion at the force with which he'd hit them, echoed through the soft summer evening, every head in the living room turned to the window.

"Here's my husband," Carol said triumphantly, relieved that he had returned to rescue her from this peculiar inquisition. "You can talk to him. You'll see how silly—" But the sentence blended into a shriek as Sheldon, paralyzed with fear, gunned the engine and zoomed off again.

The T-men jumped from their seats like so many slices of toast. Thornton called, "Let's go!" And they plummeted out of the living room and across the entrance hall. "What's going on here?" Barbara howled.

The T-man chorus poured out of the Kornpett's front

door, splitting their number between the two cars as if rehearsed, the drivers starting the motors before the doors had slammed shut. They took off out of the driveway, giving the illusion of a pack of Spitfires flying to protect London from the Luftwaffe. Curious neighbors and children stared, wide-eyed in amazement.

In the window of the colonial house, Carol and Barbara stared, too. In shock they watched the cars roar out of the driveway and carom down the quiet street, chasing . . . it was inconceivable . . . their husband and father.

"God, Mom, what is this?" Barbara asked.

Her mother turned to her, the light of sudden knowledge flicking on in her eyes. "Of course," she said quietly.

"What?"

"Who was in the basement last night?" Carol asked.

"Who?" And then the light flicked on for Barbara, too. "Oh, Jesus," she exhaled. "Mr. Ricardo."

"That crazy little bastard," Carol said, anger distorting her voice. "He's involved your father in something."

At that moment, Barbara's father was involved in turning off the quiet street and onto a busy boulevard on two wheels. It was a maneuver that would normally have scared him shitless, but this time he didn't even notice. A boiling mixture of fear and fury, he gripped the wheel with clenched fists, wrenching it this way and that as he hurtled, way above the speed limit, down what had been a boulevard of friendly shops and was now a traffic-littered maze on the road to disaster. Looking as often into the rear-view mirror as forward to the boulevard, he sped on. "I'll kill him!" he yelled to no one. "I'll tear his goddamn heart out!" Checking the mirror, he again saw the black Treasury cars, their lights blazing, cutting in and out of traffic. "Oh, God!" he cried. He pushed the accelerator to the floor, praying there were no ambulances or fire trucks coming out of any cross streets. Or cops.

"Don't lose him!" Thornton yelled to the driver in the first of the Treasury cars, as they zoomed in, out, and around traffic. The T-man felt the ride would have been more appropriate on salt flats, but smiled a little, seeing they were gaining.

They're gaining, Sheldon thought, frantic, his eyes riveted to the rear-view mirror. What if they catch me? Grabbing only instant looks at the traffic ahead, he could not keep his eyes from returning to the mirror, the sight of the big, black cars, their headlights looming always larger. I suppose my whole life should be flashing before my eyes, he thought hysterically, and obligingly, the pictures began to flash. His mother, his father, his high school graduation, that girl, what was her name? . . . under the boardwalk in Coney Island? . . . his college dorm, Carol, the army, his diploma from dental college, the wedding, Barbara in the hospital nursery puking on Carol's father, fillings, inlays, bridges, root canals, the fatal dinner party for the Ricardos, the flight down the fire escape, fainting on Mrs. Adelman, and then the headlights of the big, black cars bearing down on him inexorably.

Having brought himself back to the present, Sheldon checked the rear-view mirror again. They were closer still. He looked in front of him and saw a major intersection. Instinctively, he pulled the wheel hard and right-angled out of the lights of the pursuing cars.

The neon sign twinkled at him seductively from the top of an enormous garage roughly twenty yards down this new street.

It's an omen, he thought, and if not, what the hell? He nodded, agreeing with himself or God or whoever he thought had sent the sign. "Please, God," he whispered, in case the message had indeed come from Him, "let me get away." He turned the steering wheel sharply to the right and pulled into the automatic-paint-job garage. He pushed the shift stick up to P, took his foot off the brake pedal, allowed himself to slump back against the seat, and exhaled. Behind him, out of sight, he thought he could hear the Treasury cars hurtle by into the vast unknown reaches of New Jersey.

"Where the hell is he?" Thornton demanded of his driver. The driver, staring ahead at the traffic moving in a sedate, law-abiding manner, refused to answer. He hummed something defiantly under his breath.

"You lost him, Jerry," one of the men in back taunted the driver.

"Y'think this is easy?" Jerry demanded. He was a sore loser.

"Damn," Thornton muttered.

"You want I should go back?" Jerry asked. "Maybe check the cross streets?"

"This is Bergen County," Thornton reminded him. "Even if you know what you're looking for, you can't find it."

"Don't get mad at Jerry," the man in back threw in. "He's terrific tailing little old ladies."

"That's enough outa you, Herb," Jerry said, turning around to deliver a threatening look instead of the punch he felt Herb deserved.

"Watch it!" Thornton yelled as the car swerved dangerously near a gardening-service truck overloaded with burlaped rhododendrons. Jerry righted the car and Thornton sighed. "Just pull over wherever you can."

At the end of the block, Jerry pulled into a bus stop, and Herb, rolling down his window, flagged the other car behind them, which rolled up and double-parked. Thornton got out, moved around the two cars, and spoke to the other driver.

"We lost him," he said. "Two of you guys go back and stake out the house."

"He won't go back there," the driver said.

"I know he won't, but when I get back to headquarters, they're gonna say what happened and I'm gonna have to tell 'em Mrs. Kornpett doesn't know anything but Mr. Kornpett took off like a bat out of hell when he saw our cars. Then they're going to say"—he spoke patiently, as to a child—" 'Did you chase him?' And I'm going to say, 'Yes, but we lost him.' And they're going to say, 'So what did you do then?' and I better have an answer. And that answer is going to be, 'I staked out his house.' You, Daly"—he picked the driver—"and Turin"—he gestured to one of the men in back—"get back there."

"I got a tennis court booked at nine," Turin complained.

"I don't care if you got Farrah Fawcett booked on a leaky water bed, go stake out Kornpett's house. And get another car. One that isn't marked." Angry, he spun around and walked back to his own car. "Home, James," he told Jerry, and sank down in the seat as the car began moving. Just how important is this case, he wondered. Big enough to get me demoted to the mail room?

Gently, almost tentatively, like an insecure woman leaving the hospital after cosmetic surgery, the late-model BMW rolled out of the paint-job garage. It seemed to be asking, will anybody like me now that I'm coral-colored? And the flame decals? The ones I had engraved on my doors and windows—yes, they're indelible—are they too large? Tell the truth, now, are they just a wee bit too much?

Sheldon got out of the car and stared at it as though he were the car's husband, opposed to the surgery, wanting the familiar, saggy, pouchy beloved face back again. Near tears, he thought, I loved you. You were perfect for me. You had just the understated elegance every dentist wants in a car. Now you're a pimpmobile.

A teen-aged boy approached the car carrying a buff rag. "Beautiful job, isn't it?" he asked. He was either truly impressed or very well indoctrinated in salesman-hype for one so young. "That's thirty bucks," he said, getting down to business. "You can pay me; my dad's having supper."

Sheldon, who had been wondering if, in order to drive the car now, he would have to wear high-heeled boots and a gold lamé trench coat, turned and looked at the boy. Numbly, he withdrew his wallet and handed the kid three tens.

"It's worth it, man, believe me," the boy said. "That's

a quality paint job; it never wears out and you can't paint over it."

Oh, God, Sheldon thought, I never bought it. It's a long-term lease! What if they won't take it back? The boy was still looking at him, so Sheldon nodded. "You have a phone?" he asked.

"What?" the boy asked as if he'd never heard of one.

Somehow the boy's stupidity got to Sheldon. He flew into a sudden rage, grabbing the boy by his T-shirt and lifting him into the air. "Phone!"

"Over there," the boy cried in alarm, and the nut dropped him back on his heels and headed for the phone.

"Medium-rare okay for everybody?" Vince asked, his face under the chef's hat peering out of the smoke of the barbecue grill in the backyard.

Vickie, his guest, his neighbor, sang out, "Well for me, Vince." She and her husband were sitting at the white table on the white chairs, the striped upholstery of which matched the umbrella over the table.

"You asked for it, you got it," Vince replied, wiping his hands on his apron, which read, *I'm loaded with options*.

Jean smiled at her husband in the deepening twilight. She loved entertaining in the summer when they could take their guests out in the back of the house and she didn't have to dust the living room. Actually, she hated Vince's hamburgers, but they were better than her having to cook. "It's so nice having Vince around for a couple of days," she told Vickie and her husband, Al. She owed them three dinners and a cocktail party, and even this informal gathering was a help.

106

"It took a wedding to do it," Al was saying as though he thought it was funny.

"What did you think of Tommy's new in-laws?" Vickie asked the chef.

"Delightful," he answered immediately. "Wonderful, wonderful people. I had this instant chemical reaction, y'know, that these are really special people."

The telephone rang. "I'll get it," Jean said.

"No," Vince snapped, then more calmly, explained, "I'm expecting a call from Zurich, honey. You mind the chow." He handed her the spatula and walked toward the screened-in porch as the phone rang again. Picking up his pace, wondering what else could have happened, hoping maybe it was those handicapped people who sold light bulbs by phone, he ran onto the porch and grabbed the phone on the third ring. "Hello?" he said.

It was the voice of a raving lunatic that came back to him across the wires. A lunatic, yes; raving, certainly; but also, underneath, he could recognize the sound of Tommy's wonderful, wonderful future father-in-law.

"I've got flames on my car!" As if the voice knew that Vince could not know what the hell it was saying, it repeated, higher-pitched, more urgently, "I've got FLAMES on my car!"

Alarmed, Vince carried the phone a little deeper into the porch, checking Jean and the couple in the yard, not wanting them to be able to overhear him. They seemed to be laughing and talking, not interested in his call. It was safe to answer.

"Shelley," he said into the phone, "You're very excited. I don't know what—" He paused as a gabble of hysterical words smashed against his ear. "Who?" he asked, then mumbled, "Holy Christ! They chased you? Ah, Shel . . ."

Again the voice on the other end of the line interrupted him babbling incoherently, the word "flames" somehow leaping from the muddy torrent of words.

"I don't understand what you're saying about these flames." Vince paused and Shelley shifted gears to some hard facts. "No!" Vince cried. "No, don't go back home under any circumstances. If it's really the Treasury, you'll get arrested. Definitely."

The heat of the conversation was turning the phone booth in the garage into a sweat box. "What do I do, Vince?" Sheldon was asking desperately, realizing the idiocy of asking the source of the worst trouble of his life for advice, but having no one else to ask. "I don't want to go to jail. The wedding . . ." He paused, as Vince interrupted with an irrelevant question. Why argue, he thought, and checked his watch. "A quarter past seven," he told Vince.

Back on the porch, Vince's eyes flicked this way and that above the receiver as he feverishly sorted out his options. Keeping his voice as reassuring as possible, he spoke automatically. "Okay. Let's just stay calm and composed and this'll all work out fine." Then he made a decision. "Have you got it with you? The black bag?" he asked.

"Of course I've got the black bag," Sheldon screamed. "If I didn't have it with me, would my car be in flames?"

"Okay, okay, Shelley. Don't be nervous." Vince tried to sound as comforting as a psychiatrist in a TV drama. "Shel, what I'd like very much for you to do as soon as you hang up is drive like a bat out of hell down to

McGraw Airfield in New Jersey . . . It's near Lodi off Route 46. Bring the black bag and I'll be waiting."

"Airfield? The word reverberated around the phone booth. "You're going where?" Sheldon could hardly believe his ears. Again. "Scranton, Pennsylvania? For what?"

As quietly as possible, as though he had a lion loose from the zoo on the other end of the wire, Vince said, "I just gotta go there for a coupla hours. If you want to join me . . ."

"I don't understand," Sheldon said. "What about the Treasury Department?" The answer seemed to reinfuriate him. "Don't tell me not to worry," he yelled, loud enough for Vince to hear him without the phone. "They're chasing me all over New Jersey!"

"Shel, come with me to Scranton. By the time you get back, this'll be resolved. Take my word for it." Vince heard his wife call and turned in her direction.

"The hamburgers are ready," Jean said.

Vince held up his hand to Jean, indicating he'd be there in a minute. Then, lowering his voice, he spoke into the phone again. "Shel, the end is in sight, I assure you. Now take off . . . McGraw Airfield, just off Route 46. There'll be signs. Just follow 'em." He paused, said, "Right," paused again, and said, "Now c'mon. Let's get going."

Vince depressed the phone button with his finger, waited a second, lifted it again and heard a dial tone. Quickly he dialed another number, smiling over his shoulder reassuringly at his guests. In another second he heard the phone uncradled and now, not worried that he might be overheard, he began speaking rapidly. In Chinese.

Sheldon slammed the receiver back on the hook. "I'm not going to Scranton," he told the phone. Through the glass door of the booth he saw the kid, cringing behind the car, staring at him. "I've got to stop talking to myself," he said aloud, smoothed down his hair, and took a deep breath. "I'm not going to Scranton," he said. "I'm going to drive to McGraw Airfield and find that fink and hand him that little black bag and then go home, and if I can beat my way through the Treasury Department and probably the police and doubtless the Mafia who are surrounding my house, I will rescue Carol and . . ." For a moment he considered just leaving Barbara, who had, after all, brought all this on him, but realizing she was his only child, he thought better of it and continued: "And Barbara. Then I will drive to Kennedy Airport and if the CIA hasn't stopped my credit cards, we will all fly to wherever it was Vesco went where there is no extradition and I'll open a new practice. And I will stop talking to myself." He straightened his tie and came out of the phone booth.

There was no way Sheldon could avoid looking at his car. "Oh God," he whispered involuntarily, struck again with the horror of the paint job. The boy, keeping the car between them, made a nervous move in the direction of the door. Sheldon looked at him. "Which is the nearest back road to Lodi?" he asked.

"I don't know, mister," the boy gulped. "And my dad is having supper."

Sheldon nodded and started for the car. The boy gasped and jumped back. "I bear you no ill will," Sheldon said magnanimously and, sticking his hand into the flames, opened the door and got in. The boy was still staring at him openmouthed as he drove out of the garage.

110

He turned off the boulevard at the first cross street, feeling as conspicuous as he had once in a dream when, stark naked, he had accepted the Implant Award from the American Dental Association. I will have to take back roads even if I don't know them, he told himself, as he drove slowly down some unknown suburban street. It's not only that the Treasury Department may still be looking for me; suppose I was seen in this pimpmobile by one of the neighbors. Or a patient!

There were tears streaming from his eyes as he tried to read unfamiliar street signs in the gathering dusk on his way to McGraw Airfield.

Vince cradled the phone, took a minute to pull himself together and manufacture a story, crossed the porch, and went back out into the yard. He crossed to the picnic table, picked up a hamburger on a bun, and took a large bite out of it.

"Listen," he said to Al and Vickie, not especially wanting to look at Jean right this minute, "I know you folks'll excuse me, but something just came up."

"What is it now?" His wife's voice cut across the apologetic look he was giving his guests.

"It's a little overdone," he said, waving his hamburger at Jean. He turned back to the guests. "It'll just take me an hour or so."

"Remember, the wedding is Sunday morning," Jean said, definitely annoyed.

"I said an hour . . . two at the worst," Vince snapped.

"Was it the call from Zurich?" Vickie wanted to know.

"Yeah," he sighed. To make it good, he added, "The ambassador asked me to do him this big personal favor, so I gotta drive over to New York. To the German Embassy. Maybe you'll still be here when I get back." He jammed what was left of the hamburger into his mouth, picked up another, kissed Jean on the cheek. "Did you tell Tommy to pick up that bag from Barbara?" he asked around the burger.

"Yes," Jean answered shortly, her look telling him how annoyed and embarrassed she was.

"He doesn't have to anymore."

"I can't get him now. He went to pick up his suit . . . for the wedding," she underlined. "He's going on from there."

"No sweat," Vince said, waved his hamburger to the yard and said, "See ya later," and walked toward the Coupe de Ville parked in front of the house.

"But Al," Vickie whispered to her husband, "why's he going to the German Embassy? Zurich's in Switzerland, isn't it?"

9

By the time Sheldon reached the airfield, only a hairline separated the sun from the horizon. The sun was a huge red ball that sprayed the sky, the polluted clouds, and the very air around Sheldon's pimpmobile as from an aerosol can marked *Blood Orange*.

Sheldon drove along beside a runway till he came to a sign reading *Overnight Parking—Visitors' Parking,* with arrows pointing right and left. "Visitor," he told the sign and pulled the wheel to the right. "I am definitely a visitor." He drove a little farther and, following another arrow, pulled into a parking lot. Seeing a car back out of a parking place, he braked, waited a moment, and drove into the empty slot. A child in the back of the departing car was pointing at the pimpmobile and laughing.

Sheldon took the black bag, opened the door, pushed down the lock button, got out of the car, and slammed the door. He checked the parking meter, saw there was another seventeen minutes to go on the other guy's quarter; made a hasty calculation, and decided to be on the safe side. He inserted a quarter of his own, twisted the lever, checked that there were forty-seven minutes to go and, hefting the bag, which was heavier than it looked, started for the terminal building.

He saw Vince almost at once, standing near an information counter, drinking from a plastic cup. As Sheldon walked toward his almost-in-law, the man turned, smiled warmly, and rushed to meet him, dropping the cup in an ashtray on his way.

"Shelley," he said, as though he hadn't seen him since college, "I'm so glad you could make it."

"Yeah," Sheldon said noncommittally and handed Vince the bag. In one movement, Vince took the bag with his left hand and clutched Sheldon firmly on his bicep with his right.

"You ever been in an executive jet before, Shelley? I'm tellin' ya, believe me, it's the only way to travel."

"I'm not going anywhere," Sheldon said, as he was hustled toward an exit at the far end of the terminal.

"Just a little hop over to Scranton," Vince said, his hand pincerlike on Shelley's arm. "Y'ever been there? What a great little town. You'll relax. We'll be home in an hour."

"I don't want to go to Scranton," Sheldon said, trying to get his arm back.

"Listen, I'll buy you dinner. There is a restaurant in Scranton," Vince was selling hard, "an Indonesian restaurant . . ."

"In Scranton?"

"Refugees," Vince explained. "They make a bird's-nest soup that'll knock your socks off."

"Bird's-nest soup? That's Chinese." Sheldon realized he was outside again. They were walking toward a small airplane alone on the end of a runway. Its engine was on and whining.

"Well," Vince explained, hurrying him along, "it's an Indonesian restaurant but they have a Chinese cook. Chang Hoo. What a terrific guy. See?" he said as he shoved Sheldon up three steps to the door of the plane. "We're all ready to go."

"I don't want to go to Scranton. I don't like bird's-nest soup." Sheldon pulled his arm away and made a determined stand on the top step.

Vince looked injured. "An hour. Two hours if we stop to eat. Please let me buy you a meal," he begged.

"But I only put a quarter in the meter," Sheldon argued and, checking his watch, added, "In thirty-nine minutes, I'll get a parking ticket."

"Shelley," Vince dismissed the problem, "this is New Jersey. All the cops are corrupt." He pushed his reluctant guest into the plane.

Sheldon turned back to the door, but a Chinese gentleman who seemed to have appeared from nowhere was pulling up the steps and shutting the door. As Sheldon watched he took up a guardlike position, arms akimbo, in front of it.

"I'd like ya to meet Bing Wong," Vince said. "This is Dr. Sheldon Kornpett, beyond question the finest dentist in the city of New York. The man is an artist with his spritz drill." Having given Sheldon's credits, his tone became more prosaic. "Sit down, Shelley," he said and started toward the pilot's cabin.

"Where are you going?" Sheldon had the distinct impression he did not want to be left alone with the Oriental gentleman.

"Cockpit," Vince answered.

"You're not going to drive!"

"Just for the takeoff," Vince said, opening the cockpit curtain.

"But . . ."

"Then I let my copilot take over. Billy Wong. Bing's brother. Charming guy."

"But . . ." Sheldon said. He had no idea of what he would say next even if Vince let him get in a full sentence.

"Soon as we're in the air, I'll come back to the cabin and you and I can have a nice shmooze." With that Vince disappeared into the cockpit and Sheldon turned back to the door, wondering if there was any point in trying to scream "Help!" over the sound of the airplane.

Bing Wong was still in place.

"Nice to meet you," Sheldon said automatically.

Bing Wong smiled down at Sheldon and said something in Chinese that sounded like "Fasten your seat belt."

In the cockpit, Vince settled himself in the pilot's chair beside his middle-aged Chinese copilot. He smiled his hello, fastened his seat belt, and then addressed a question to the man in Chinese. Billy Wong answered; Vince nodded his understanding and flicked a switch on the instrument panel before him. The plane's windshield wiper went on. Vince said, "That's wrong," and looked embarrassed.

In the passenger section, rapidly appproaching catatonia,

Sheldon had dumped himself into a seat and was struggling to fasten the seat belt with fingers that were suddenly the consistency of cold spaghetti.

Before him stood the large Chinese gentleman giving the safety spiel with the smiling assurance of a TWA stewardess who had just returned from a refresher course at charm school. He waved the instruction card under Sheldon's nose, dropped the oxygen mask and pulled it over his face, demonstrating how to breathe. Then he materialized a life jacket from somewhere and showed Sheldon how to put it on. Through it all he kept up a cheerful explanation of his activities in Chinese.

I'm insane, Sheldon thought in English.

In the cockpit, Vince pulled a lever and the engine speed increased.

In the cabin, Sheldon heard Vince's voice on the intercom say, "Will the flight attendant please be seated?" and watched as the big Chinese gentleman hastened to a seat across the aisle and strapped himself in. Sheldon felt the plane move, begin to pick up ground speed in preparation for liftoff. It was only when he glanced out of the window that he realized the plane was moving in reverse. Obviously Vince, out of sight at the controls, noticed at the same moment, and with an agonized screech of tires, the plane stopped abruptly.

"Just getting us into position," that voice said over the intercom, and Sheldon realized that for the umpteenth time that day he was praying under his breath. There are no atheists in foxholes, he thought, and none that get involved with Vince Ricardo either.

The plane began to move forward, smoothly this time,

and though Sheldon had shut his eyes, he sensed the liftoff and knew the plane was airborne.

The two men sat silent in the car parked on the quiet street about fifty yards from the colonial house. They had been there over an hour and conversation had flagged. At one point Turin had turned the radio on to a top-fifty station and Daly had immediately turned it off. They had not spoken since, except when Daly rolled down his window and yelled at a woman for allowing her schnauzer to urinate on the front wheel.

"Y'think he coulda gotten here before we did?" Daly suddenly broke the silence.

"Nah," his companion answered. "Where's his car?"

"Garage?"

"Nah."

"The Toyota's still in front," Daly pointed out.

Turin looked at him. "With your sense of observation, you should go in for detective work," he said.

They settled into silence again.

After about ten minutes a Volkswagen pulled into the block and the two Treasury men watched as it slowed down and parked at the curb in front of the colonial house.

"That him?" Daly wondered.

"Ain't his car," Turin said, and, seeing a young man get out, he added, "and that ain't him."

They watched as the young man walked up the Kornpett driveway and rang the bell. When the door opened and he went inside, Turin said, "Get his license number."

"Probably the girl's boyfriend," Daly answered.

"He's still got a license. Get it," Turin replied.

Daly opened the car door, looked back, and asked,

118

"Who appointed you general?" He got out and sauntered as inconspicuously as possible down the dark street till he could see the license number, and wrote it down on the back of an envelope. On the way back he stepped in some dog dirt.

"Christ," he said, getting back into the car.

"You're smellin' up the whole car," Turin complained.

Ripping the number off the envelope, Daly used the remainder to try to clean his shoe. "I live in New York," he said. "Don't they have doggie scoops in New Jersey?" He threw the dirtied envelope out of the car.

When the wild departure of the Treasury Department men chasing Sheldon was over, Barbara and Carol had both been too nervous, too frightened to eat. After half an hour of pacing and staring at the phone, they had decided to have tea. They wound up eating a small wheel of Edam cheese, half a box of Ritz crackers, and four cinnamon buns they found in the freezer.

They spent another half-hour raging against Vince Ricardo and wondering where Sheldon was. They they each had several Maalox tablets.

"If they caught him, we'd've heard," Barbara said, considering what to eat to rid her mouth of the chalky Maalox taste.

"If they didn't catch him, where is he?" her mother countered. "And besides that, what did he do?"

"He didn't even know about the engraving in the basement."

"Then why did he run away?" Carol demanded.

They looked at each other for a long moment, both understanding that only one person could answer the question but neither of them wanting to be the one who said it. Finally Carol could stand it no more. "Vince would know why," she announced.

Barbara shrugged and nodded, not wanting to admit that it was true but also not wanting to look like an idiot by denying the obvious.

Carol looked a long question at Barbara, who finally rose and went to the telephone. She picked up the receiver, then put it down. "Just suppose," she said. "Suppose he doesn't know."

"That's not possible," Carol said firmly.

"But if . . ." Barbara insisted. "Do I want my father-in-law to know that my father is a fugitive from justice?"

Carol considered the problem. "It's no way to start a marriage," she admitted at last.

"No," Barbara agreed.

They decided their best move was to have a glass of white wine.

At last, Barbara persuaded her mother to take a long, relaxing bath and even volunteered some of the bath salts she had been saving for her honeymoon. Promising she would not leave the phone in case Daddy called, Barbara had gotten Carol into the tub and was just coming back downstairs when the doorbell rang.

"What's the matter?" Tommy asked, seeing her face when she opened the door.

"Nothing," Barbara answered and, closing the door, fell into his arms sobbing.

"Who is that?" Carol called from upstairs.

"Tommy," Barbara yelled back.

"There is something the matter," Tommy said.

"No," Barbara said.

"We're going to the movies," Tommy called up the stairs to her mother.

"Movies!" was the shocked reply from upstairs, and "Movies?" the question from the girl in his arms.

"Don't you remember? The motel movies?" Tommy said.

"Oh, Tommy," Barbara said, flustered, having forgotten in the excitement.

"You told me," Tommy reminded her.

"Oh yes," she said, trying to recover.

"Don't you want to?" he asked. "What's the matter?"

"Certainly I want to. Nothing's the matter," she said and kissed him. She knew suddenly she wanted to be with him; more than anything in the world she wanted to feel his arms around her, to take comfort and escape from this insane day in the act of love. I guess that's what love's about, she thought. "I'll just go tell Mother," she whispered and went back up the stairs.

"I'm just going to the movies with Tommy," she said loud enough for him to hear from in front of the bathroom door.

"How can you go to the movies at a time like this?" Carol hissed from among the soap suds.

"Well, I promised. And if I don't," Barbara hissed back, "then I'll have to tell him why."

"Can't you say you have a sick headache?"

"That's no way to start a marriage either!"

Carol sat back in the tub. She realized that her daughter, whatever she said, was not going to the movies.

"I hate to leave you alone," Barbara said in a normal tone of voice.

"Where's your father?" Tommy called from the bottom of the stairs.

"He went out," Barbara called back.

"All right," Carol said, figuring there was nothing the girl could do anyway, and why shouldn't she get whatever she could out of life considering how anyone could find an engraving for a five-hundred-dollar bill anytime in their basement. And have the Treasury Department and God knows who chasing them at any moment. "Just wait till I get out of the tub so I can answer the phone," she said, rising and brushing soap bubbles from her body as she reached for the towel.

Barbara went to her room and slipped a few things into a tote bag and went back downstairs. "I just have to wait with the phone till she gets out of the tub," she explained.

"Are you expecting a call?"

"No," she answered.

"Oh," Tommy said but decided it wasn't important. "Did your dad leave a little black bag for my father? I'm supposed to pick it up."

"He hasn't been home."

"Then how did he go out?"

"Well," Barbara paused, "he was home . . . but he didn't quite come into the house."

"Is something the matter?"

"Why?" Barbara asked.

"You're acting . . . I don't know . . . funny."

"No, I'm not," she said quickly.

"Okay. I'm out," Carol called from upstairs.

"We won't be long," Barbara called back.

"We're just going to the movies," Tommy yelled, protesting too much.

"Try *Superman*," Carol suggested coolly from above them.

"What did she mean by that?" Tommy asked as he escorted Barbara through the door.

"I don't know," she answered. Then she was silent till they were in the car and Tommy had kissed her, seriously.

"You stay here and watch the house. I'm going to tail the girl," Turin said.

"I can't just stand here and watch the house," Daly objected. "It ain't like New York. It's a street. With houses. What'll I do?"

"Get out!" Turin ordered. "I'll lose them. She may be meeting the father."

Daly got out but held the door open. "What'll I do?" he repeated.

"Hide behind a tree!" Turin snarled, pulled the door shut, and took off after the Volkswagen.

They were just turning the corner into the boulevard when Tommy's earlier question, which had been stewing in the bottom of Barbara's brain, finally percolated. "Why would your father be getting a little black bag from my father?"

"I don't know. Which motel?"

"Was it my father's bag or your father's bag?"

"How about The Bushes?"

"That's not a motel. It's a cabin camp."

"What's the difference?"

"It has those tin showers in the corner of the rooms," she said in some irritation.

"I didn't know you were going to take a shower."

"What was in the bag?" Barbara went back to what was bothering her.

"Which bag?"

"The black bag."

"Barbara, I really don't know. My mother told me he told her to tell me to pick up a bag. The place in Englewood Cliffs?"

"Too nearby."

"It has beautiful bathrooms."

"And if it was your father's bag, how did my father get it?"

"Maybe it has something to do with the wedding. A wedding present. A surprise." Mentioning the wedding, Tommy was reminded of the stirring in his groin. "Which motel?" he asked again, trying to make his irritation sound amorous.

"The one in Newburg. But if it was a wedding present and my father had it, it would have been in my house with the rest of the presents, why would your father want it?"

"To have it engraved!" he yelled, and, "Newburg is twelve miles."

"So?"

"It's in New York," the boy objected. "Across a state line." He had a feeling that was illegal.

"Pompton Lakes," Barbara said, rather than argue.

"I hope I can hold out that long," Tommy said, trying to establish a romantic atmosphere. Barabara paid no attention. He turned the car toward Route 4.

"Your father says he's a consultant."

"Why are we talking about my father?"

"What does that mean? Consultant?"

124

"It means he consults."

"With whom? About what?" Barbara asked.

Tommy felt like a fool. "Well, I don't really know."

"You don't know what your father does for a living?" she asked, a frightened feeling congealing like a storm center in her stomach.

"He's a very private person."

"Still . . ." she insisted.

"He always said he was a consultant. He travels a lot." Suddenly his tone turned from the defensive. "Why do you want to know now?"

She told him: the engraving in the basement, the scene in the bank, the mysterious Mr. Smith and the nonexistent gas meter, the Treasury Department men, and her father's peculiar arrival and departure at seven o'clock.

"And you think it has something to do with my father?" he asked when she was finished.

"It never happened before he came to our house," she said. "It never happened before he told you to pick up a black bag."

Slowly, Tommy pulled the car out of the traffic, and slid into a stop in front of a Kentucky Fried Chicken. From the past a dozen, a hundred unassorted, unconsidered impressions popped out of his memory. He had a terrible desolating feeling that maybe the girl was right. Maybe there was something illegal in what his father did. All the traveling . . . Smuggling? Narcotics? The Mafia? He is Italian, the boy thought. He turned and looked at the beautiful girl beside him and knew that he loved her and wanted her for his whole life. "I knew something was the matter," he said.

"Yes," she admitted.

"Do you want to call off the wedding?" he asked.

"Oh no!" she said. "Why would I want that?"

"Because . . . maybe my father did get you father into trouble."

"Even if he did, it's not *your* fault," she said. "Tommy, I love you. Never more than tonight. I realized when you came to the house . . . I was so upset . . . frantic . . . and when I saw you I knew that I wanted you to hold me, make love to me, that that was the most important thing in the world to me." She kissed him, hard, pressing her body into his. "Oh, Tommy," she said, "forget Pompton Lakes. Just drive to The Bushes."

"It's not the time, Barbara," he said, an hereditary guilt pressing on him.

"Please."

"No."

"Why not?"

"I don't think we should."

"You don't want to," Barbara said. She had the strange feeling she had had this whole conversation before.

"I do. You know how much I do."

"Then, why not?"

"Because I don't think we should."

Barbara remembered the whole conversation. They had had it two nights before from opposite sides of the court. She sighed forcefully, as much to let the boy know her frustration and annoyance as to expel the air. She moved away from him and stared at the Kentucky Fried Chicken place. A man in the window stared back. She stuck out her tongue at him and he turned away.

"Barbara," the boy whispered, "I love you but this just isn't the time."

"When is?" she said sharply.

"Sunday. Like you said, at the Plaza. By then your father will be back and this whole thing will be cleared up. I'd feel guilty this way."

"Please . . ." she said.

"No," he replied.

"Why not?" she demanded again.

When they had completed the entire combination down to "Because I don't think we should," once more, Tommy turned the key in the ignition. As the car started off, Barbara, through her tears, saw the man in the Kentucky Fried Chicken grab his bucket and rush out to his car.

"I just feel funny about it now . . . knowing about your father . . . and your mother's home all alone . . ." Tommy was saying. But Barbara had squirmed round in her seat and was watching the man's car start and come after them.

"I think we're being followed," she said.

"That's impossible," Tommy answered and wondered if it was.

He drove her home in silence but noticed she turned to look out of the rear window every time he went around a corner. He parked in front of her house. "Angry?" he asked.

"No," she said angrily. "But he just parked up the block."

"Who?"

"The man who followed us."

"Nobody followed us."

"Yes, he did."

"You're being paranoid."

"Well, I can't help it. I'm not used to being followed. I don't come from a criminal background."

Tommy felt that was going too far. "Neither do I!" he yelled. "My father is an international business consultant, which is more distinguished than poking around in people's mouths."

"You don't know what your father is!"

"He's a terrific guy. A little tense but terrific."

"If your father is legit, why is the Treasury Department chasing my father? Why are we being followed?"

Tommy took a deep breath. "I don't want to fight," he said, controlling his voice. "I just want to think about Sunday. I can't wait for Sunday." He modulated down to what he hoped was an insinuating, erotic tone of voice.

"I wish that was true," Barbara snapped, feeling rejected, frustrated, and followed.

"What do you mean by that?"

"I mean any man whose fiancée practically threw herself at him and he didn't take her up on it . . . well, I don't know . . ."

"Are you implying there's something wrong with me?"

"How would I know?" Barbara snarled. "You never really do know till after the wedding, do you?"

"You want to call off the wedding?"

"I can't. My mother asked the whole family. And you know what a nasty mouth my Aunt Louise has!"

"That's no reason for not getting married!"

"I can't not get married," Barbara howled, upset and just going with the flow. "If you want to not get married, we'll do it after the wedding!" She jumped out of the car and ran up the driveway.

"Okay," he yelled after her. "If that's the way you feel

about it!" He waited until she had opened the door and gone in without apologizing.

"That was some quick movie," Carol said, coming out of the kitchen.

"Yes," Barbara answered and went down the steps into the living room.

Her mother followed her. She thought, Too quick a movie or whatever. She tried to remember how she had taught Sheldon to slow down and whether to discuss it mother-daughter style.

"Did Daddy call?" Barbara asked. She lifted the curtain of the French window in the darkened living room and looked out.

"No," her mother said. Barbara saw Tommy's car moving down toward the end of the street and looked back toward the other car. She saw a bucket of chicken fly out of the open door and be caught by someone standing behind a tree. Then the car door slammed and it sped down the street after Tommy.

"I'm frightfully worried," the two women said at the same time.

Sheldon had to admit that it had been, since the takeoff, a smooth flight, although he still hadn't opened his eyes. He estimated they had been airborne half an hour and decided to risk looking at his watch. Slowly, he opened his eyes and stared at his wrist. It had been only ten minutes. Tentatively he moved his head to look around the cabin. Vince was nowhere to be seen. Bing Wong was strapped in across the aisle further back in the plane reading a copy of *Ebony* magazine.

Sheldon moved his head in the other direction toward

the window, and the feeling of disaster he had been waiting for struck him. They were flying over water. Lots of water. "The ocean?" he said aloud. "We go over the ocean to Scranton?" He looked back at the Chinese gentleman, who gave no sign of having heard.

In the cockpit Vince said something jovial to Billy Wong, who nodded. Vince rose and went back into the passenger section. Sheldon saw him at once.

"Shel—" Vince began, but Sheldon wasn't waiting for him.

"Why are we going over the ocean?" the dentist demanded.

"That's what I want to tell you about. There's been a slight change in our flight plan." Vince did his best to make it sound as unimportant as an off-year election, but it was not reassuring enough for his passenger.

"Not Scranton?" Sheldon howled.

"No, we're going to Scranton," Vince continued, as calm as a mother singing a lullaby. "But we have to make a quick stop somewhere else first."

"Where?"

"Honduras."

Sheldon nodded. "Honduras," he repeated, to be absolutely certain he had heard correctly.

"That's right." Vince smiled. "I think you'll find it quite fascinating . . ."

All of life is a choice, Sheldon thought. Sometimes we must choose between good things and sometimes, like now, we must choose between bad things. The thing is to choose the best good thing or the least bad thing and do it fast. Having so decided, he reached beneath his seat, grabbed the life jacket there, catapulted to his feet, and dashed madly toward the door of the plane.

Vince cried out in Chinese and the Chinese steward or pirate, or whatever he was, dropped his *Ebony* and in one lithe, athletic movement was out of his seat and had tackled Sheldon.

"I'm so terribly sorry about Vince," Jean Ricardo was saying to Al and Vickie in the front door as Tommy drove the Volkswagen into the garage. "These things just seem to come up."

"Forget it," Al said. "Thanks for a swell time."

"Your mashed-potato salad is too much," Vickie said. "And please don't worry about Vince. We understand, and he's a terrific guy." Jean smiled and closed the front door. "I think he's a crook," Vickie said under her breath to her husband as they went down the walk.

"Y'know," Al said philosophically, "I think you're right."

"You do?" Vickie asked, surprised at this unusual agreement. "Why?"

" 'Cause there's a guy sitting in a car over there watching this house," her husband said.

"Jesus!" Vickie mumbled. "You think we could get into trouble?"

"For what? For eating that God-awful mashed-potato salad?"

"Well," Vickie worried her way down the street, "there were those business deductions . . . If the IRS . . ."

"That black bag I was supposed to pick up from Barbara," Tommy was saying in the kitchen.

"Daddy said forget it," Jean said, tossing paper plates into the garbage.

"What was in it?"

"Look," Jean said, turning to her son, "I love your father. But one thing I've learned in twenty-five years of marriage is never ask what's in anything."

It was pitch-dark outside the plane window and all Sheldon could see were the reflections of red flashing lights on the wing. Pointlessly sullen, he continued to stare through the little window trying to remember exactly where Honduras was and whether it was an island. His geography from Mexico to Brazil was not too hot. Beside him sat the large Chinese gentleman, one eye on a copy of *Better Homes and Gardens*, whose pages he was flipping, the other eye on Sheldon. Turning a page and seeing something he liked, he nudged Sheldon companionably and pointed to a picture.

Sheldon turned from the window and looked at the picture, which seemed to be an arrangement of lilacs, grapefruit, and weeds. "Very lovely," he said, but he sounded discouraged. He heard a noise and looking up saw That Man come out of the cockpit. Vince addressed Sheldon's seatmate in Chinese and the man nodded, got up, and gave Vince his seat.

"Isn't he a sweetheart?" Vince asked, as if nothing was wrong. Sheldon refused to be sucked into a conversation. "You know," Vince went on, as though Sheldon had answered, "if Chiang Kai-shek had ever made it back to the mainland, Billy and Bing would have been co-anchormen on the evening news in China? That's how beloved they were."

132

Bullshit, Sheldon thought and, saying nothing, reinforced his hostility by withdrawing his gaze from Vince, turning his head and pointedly staring out the window at nothing.

"You're furious at me, right? I tricked you." Vince confronted the problem head-on, but with no more success at drawing Sheldon out. Still he plunged on in the face of his guest's total silence. "The amazing thing is how grateful you're gonna be to me when this is all over."

Amazed by the man's sheer gall, Sheldon could not refrain from shaking his head but still managed to say nothing. He continued staring out the window, half expecting to see a fire break out on the wing.

"I'm very serious," Vince went on doggedly. "From here on in, it's strictly routine. We got out of the country, we're home free. All that happens from now on—" Beginning to feel foolish conducting this one-sided conversation, he interrupted himself to ask, "Are you interested in this?"

Silence.

Vince continued anyway. "All that happens is that we're met at the airport by Senator Pat Braunschweiger, a corrupt member of the Honduras legislature. He checks out the engravings. We go to the hotel, wash up, have a couple of beers."

Sheldon restrained himself from saying, No bird's-nest soup?

"In the late afternoon, we meet with General García— the head of this Latin American syndicate. We hand him the engravings, he hands us twenty million bucks, and, bingo, we got him red-handed."

It was more than he could stand. Sheldon turned from

the window and stared at Vince. "Then what happens?" he asked quietly. "There's a big shootout?"

Vince laughed uproariously. "Shel," he said, "you've been seeing too many movies."

Sheldon did not deign to answer. I am living a movie, he thought. *The Fall of the House of Kornpett.*

10

I'm worrying about the wrong things, Carol told herself as she flopped around disconsolately in the big, half-empty double bed. I was going to worry about the wedding itself tonight and about Barbara and the marriage tomorrow night. And I hardly know how to worry about Shel. I've never had to before. "Comes through that door at seven o'clock every single night," she heard herself telling the Treasury men. And it was true. He did. And even tonight, he got as far as the front of the driveway.

She plumped up Shelley's pillow and set it beside her the long way, hoping somehow to compensate for the lack of a body next to hers. And basically, she continued to herself, I would have reorganized the worry schedule anyway after that peculiar conversation with Barbara. It was obvious that she and Tommy had had some kind of lover's squabble. Well, premarital nerves, she decided, and turned over, facing away from the pillow facsimile of her husband. But what was that about a black bag? Barbara had mentioned it but then gone on to something else. Sheldon had a black bag. Sheldon had run away with a black bag that Tommy was supposed to get for Vince. Well, if Shelley had run away with a woman, I'd know how to handle it. Or could black bag mean a black woman? . . . Oh, that's ridiculous, she told herself. If there's one thing I'm sure of, it's that Sheldon is faithful to me. Then why wouldn't Barbara discuss the black bag? Because she doesn't know anything about it.

But why didn't Shelley call?

Obviously, because he couldn't.

Why?

Kidnapped? Drugged? Dead?

Carol began to cry. Should I have called his family, she wondered. No. His sister Louise would drive me up the wall. I am up the wall. The first thing she'd imply is that Shelley ran off with a woman. "Well, he didn't!" she screamed into the darkened room. "He ran off with a black bag!"

Oh God, she thought. What if he doesn't get back for the wedding? Well, if I hear from him, he'll tell me what to do. If I don't hear from him, what do I do? Do I go on with it? Or cancel it? Then what do I do with all those hors d'oeuvres? There isn't a freezer in Teaneck big enough to . . .

This is nonsense. My husband has been kidnapped, or worse, and I'm worrying about hors d'oeuvres. At least

Rubin's Catering takes back the champagne. And with all those men running around the house, I never got my half-slip, and Oh! She sat up, remembering the worst. I never got Shelley's suit back from the cleaners.

Oh God, she thought, tossing herself back down on the pillows, even if he comes back for the wedding, he'll have to go in his underwear.

Down the hall, Barbara sat crosslegged on the medium-sized four-poster bed she had slept in since high school, a doll from the primordial days before kindergarten in her lap. Having long since given up the idea of sleeping, she was playing a complicated solitaire involving two decks of cards and complete stoppage of the circulation in her legs.

What's the matter with Tommy? she thought. I couldn't have been more specific about what I wanted tonight short of unzipping his fly. I thought any man . . . except . . . could he be . . . ? Oh, that's ridiculous and you know it! And I wouldn't do it Wednesday and he didn't think I was a . . . or did he? Is that why he wanted to call off the wedding? Why didn't I do it Wednesday? I wanted to. Why didn't he want to do it tonight? He wanted to. Well, he was upset. He was upset for me, she decided, which somehow made it worse. Because my father—

Not wanting to continue the thought and having come to the end of the double pack of cards, she smooshed the unsuccessful solitaire together, stacked the cards, shuffled, and dealt a new game.

Where's Daddy? she wondered. What has that fiend Vince Ricardo done with him? If Daddy's . . . She backed away from a very unpleasant word and started again. If something has happened to Daddy, can I still marry Tommy? Would I want to? Could I marry him on condition that we never speak to his father again? Would Tommy agree?

And can Mom get through the wedding the way things are? Can I? She had finished setting up the solitaire and looked at her bedside clock. It was three A.M. She rose, careful not to disturb the cards, and went to her dressing-table mirror and looked at the haggard face in it. All brides are beautiful, she thought. Well, that's one cliché I can disprove on Sunday. If there is a wedding. If there is a Sunday. She went back to the bed and swept the cards to the floor in one extravagant gesture, then grabbed the doll and threw herself onto the bed. "I want Tommy," she said to the doll. "I need him. And I still need shoes, too."

The kitchen clock said three-thirty and Tommy was making instant pudding. It was perfectly logical, he thought; the other kind of pudding takes too long and there was absolutely nothing in the fridge he wanted to eat and nerves made him hungry. At three-thirty-two he figured he had mixed the pudding enough, and he looked back at the instructions on the box. They said let it stand for five minutes, but at this hour of the night he felt that was a waste of time. Eventually he had to get to bed. He needed his rest, needed his strength for Sunday night. Especially after what happened tonight. Nothing happened, he reminded himself. What the hell was the matter with me? She was kissing me, on top of me, I love her. I'm a fool.

He took the entire bowl and the soup spoon he had used to mix the pudding and sat at the kitchen counter. On the

138

first mouthful he knew it was grainy, uncoagulated, and *yich*. But on the other hand, it was chocolate, so he went on eating. Barbara needed comfort. Her father was missing. But on the other hand, so was his father, and Barbara said very nasty things about him and about me. She implied I was less than a man, and only 'cause I wouldn't take her to a motel, and I guess she was right.

I wonder if Sheldon Kornpett got home? Vince isn't home but that's not unusual. Could Barbara be right? Is there something illegal about the old man? What if there is? He's still my father. Doesn't he pay my tuition? What if he got sent to jail? What would Mom do? Who would pay my tuition? Would the Bar Association let me in if my father was in the slammer?

"Jesus," he muttered, scraping the bowl with the spoon, licking the spoon, and throwing it back into the bowl. I'm too young to cope with all this. I'm too young to get married. I'm too young . . . but the thought of Barbara in a nightgown that could barely hang onto her shoulders, sprawled luxuriously on a bed in the Plaza Hotel Sunday night, lifting her arms to him, her lips gently forming his name . . . He felt an instantaneous stirring down in his pajama bottoms and automatically reached down for himself.

No, he thought, I'm too old for that.

On the floor above Tommy, Jean Ricardo slept peacefully. To be sure, when she went to bed she was annoyed that Vince had spoiled her little cookout for Vickie and Al, but as for the wedding, he'd get there. He always managed somehow. And as for Vince not being there in her bed? On the whole she preferred it. He tended to kick in his sleep.

James Thornton of the United States Treasury Department did not sleep that night either. Nor did his superior, who thoroughly enjoyed himself reaming Thornton out for losing the prime suspect in the biggest case of the decade.

"I've still got leads," was all Thornton could think of to say in his own defense as he hoped against hope that those two meatheads, Daly and Turin, had come up with something on their stakeout.

Turin came up with nothing but a large pain in the neck, having fallen asleep in a cramped position in his car in front of the Ricardo house. Daly came up with a large pile of chicken bones and a summer cold.

Vince slept like a baby.

Sheldon, sure he was facing certain death at the hands of this lunatic, had refused to speak to him anymore. As the evening wore on and the plane flew southward, he surreptitiously watched as first Vince and then Bing Wong fell asleep in the passenger cabin. When he was sure they had gone off, Sheldon once again considered jumping, but he realized that unlike his earlier attempt off Jersey where he knew the waters . . . sort of . . . he was now farther south. With my luck, he decided, I would jump straight into the Bermuda Triangle.

Shortly thereafter, worn out by the physical and emotional stresses of the day, he fell into a troubled sleep.

The airfield at Tegucigalpa, Honduras, did not exactly

bustle. It lay there, comatose in the tropic heat. The terminal building boasted no Executive Lounge, no restaurant, no duty-free shops. There was a dirty unisex toilet and a broken Coke machine.

Sunrise was the slow time of day at the airport. The palm trees shifted in the wind; they almost seemed to scratch themselves and roll over. If, as occasionally happened, a coconut fell from one, it detonated with an excitement comparable to a bomb at O'Hare or the arrival of the Pope or Liza Minelli at Kennedy. The grass, which could hardly be separated from the tarmac, and frequently wasn't, was wet with dew. The skies were cloudless. The few small private aircraft parked around the strip rusted quietly.

For an average iguana who happened to be passing by on this particular morning, there was only one unusual sight. It was a gray Mercedes 450 SEL parked near the landing strip, though it is doubtful that the iguana could identify it. He might, however, have recognized the figure leaning against the door of the Mercedes as human.

Nothing in the world could get Senator Pat Braunschweiger out of bed before dawn except money. But money, in great quantities, had brought the trim and elegant senator, immaculately tailored as usual, to this pretty pass. He stood, furious at being kept waiting, nervously smoking a cigarette, occasionally scanning the blue and cloudless sky.

The iguana, who had not yet breakfasted, and was looking for something to eat, was distracted by the sound of an approaching airplane, which, though he had lived near the airport his entire life, frightened him. The sound had the opposite effect, one of relief, on the senator. He squinted up into the sky and smiled, seeing the silver sides of the aircraft glinting in the rising sun.

The iguana, the search for peace and privacy taking precedence over breakfast, skittered up the hillside directly behind him. He was making a dreadful mistake. Up there, half buried in the heavy vegetation on the side of the hill, was another car, a black sedan which, like the iguana and Honduras, had seen better days. Three men in business suits were seated on its roof. All three were watching the airstrip. One, Edgardo, through binoculars, the other two, Alfonso and Carlos, through the telescopic sights of their rifles. The iguana, who was not too smart, hid himself behind a rock. If he'd eaten and had been thinking better, he would have gotten the hell out of there.

"Mira! Aeroplano!" one of the three on top of the car whispered. The other two looked quickly to the big silver bird, then back down to the airstrip. Edgardo followed the swooping descent of the plane, cutting like a machete through the soft daybreak air, coming at last to earth, rising slightly, coming to earth again and rising slightly again. After a few more bounces, the plane ground to a complete halt.

From the top of their half-hidden car, the three men watched Senator Braunschweiger throw his cigarette to the ground and walk briskly toward the plane.

Relieved, and somewhat surprised, to be on the ground again, even if the ground was Honduras, Sheldon unstrapped himself and followed Vince to the door of the plane. Bing Wong had already opened it, and his brother, the copilot, had come from the cockpit to bid them farewell. In the open door, Vince embraced both the Wong brothers and kissed them on both cheeks. He then made

142

a short speech in Chinese, evidently thanking them for the flight. The brothers bowed and smiled at Vince; then all three turned to Sheldon.

I will not kiss a Chinese pilot, Sheldon thought. It's not that I'm prejudiced against Orientals, I just don't go around kissing pilots. However, since something was obviously required of him, he smiled and bowed as the two men had done and nodded toward Vince. "What he said," he told them, as graciously as possible.

Vince smiled. "Very nice, Shel," he said, as though Sheldon had successfully given a blessing at a UN dinner. Then he turned to the door, said, "Okey-doke, let's move," and led the way out of the plane, carrying the little black bag.

Following Vince down the three short steps, Sheldon got only a vague impression of the airstrip. It looked to him like something the Marines had built on Iwo Jima thirty-five years ago and abandoned six months later. He wondered how the plane had managed to land at all. Behind him he could hear the sound of the steps from the airplane retracting and realized the motor had not been turned off. Were the Chinese pilots leaving them here? Alone? In Honduras? And I don't even really know it is Honduras, he thought, evaluating how reliable Vince had been up to now. Considering the palm trees, he decided it certainly wasn't Scranton. His attention was diverted by a trim, elegantly dressed gentleman walking toward them across the tarmac, his arms outstretched in greeting.

On the hillside only Edgardo was watching the senator through his field glasses. Carlos and Alfonso had momentarily stopped staring at him through their rifle sights in order to cock their rifles.

"Pat!" Vince cried, giving every evidence of delight at seeing Senator Braunschweiger.

"This guy's a crook?" Sheldon whispered beside him as they crossed the field.

"They're all crooks down here," Vince replied. "At least this one don't make any bones about it."

Senator Braunschweiger, beaming, his arms open wide in greeting, strode up to them. "Welcome to Honduras," he cried. At that, a barrage of gunfire cut short his greeting and his life. The dapper, well-dressed gentleman fell to the ground in a heap before them.

"Hit the dirt!" Vince advised, hurling himself to the tarmac.

Sheldon did not need urging and dropped close beside Vince as more bullets hurtled past them. Had one hit him, Sheldon would hardly have noticed, so numb with terror was he. "Is he dead?" he gasped.

"If he's alive, he's puttin' on some fuckin' act, ain't he?" Vince growled into the hail of bullets that continued around them. Then he barked, "Roll over!"

Sheldon, having little experience in this kind of situation, did as he was told. In the middle distance he saw the plane begin to taxi away.

"They're leaving us to die," he screamed.

"That's standard procedure," Vince told him.

"What?" Sheldon could not believe his ears. Or his eyes. Or anything else.

"We gotta make a run for the car," Vince decided.

"We'll never make it." Sheldon hated being negative, but after all, there was no cover on the bare airfield.

"We ain't gonna make it lying here, that's for goddamn sure," Vince snapped. "You ready?"

"No!"

Another round of bullets came close enough to bounce dirt into their faces.

"Now I'm ready," Sheldon said.

Vince nodded and rose, keeping his chunky, compact body in a crouch, and started running toward the Mercedes. Sheldon, feeling that he did not want to be left alone in a strange country, followed a split-second behind.

"Serpentine!" Vince yelled over the splat-splat of gunfire.

"What?"

"Serpentine!" He yelled louder and made a gesture with his hand to indicate that Sheldon should run in a curving pattern. Sheldon agreed immediately and began zigzagging, finding it easier on the rough, untended airstrip than trying to lurch along in a straight line.

Up on the hillside, their rifles weaving along with the targets, Carlos and Alfonso fired and cursed, cursed and fired.

Sheldon and Vince, sweating in the cool of the early morning, miraculously reached the car, whipped open the doors, and jumped in. Sheldon sat in the passenger seat, gasping for breath, as Vince, behind the wheel, searched madly for the keys.

"Where the hell are the keys?" he asked as though Sheldon would know.

"You're kidding me," suggested the dentist frantically, as a burst of gunfire shattered the rear window.

"Out of the car!" Vince ordered, and they dived from the Mercedes, rolling on the ground, the auto between them and the vicious barrage from the hillside.

"They have to be in his pocket," Sheldon said logically, amazed at his powers of deduction under fire.

"I'll get 'em," Vince said and started to rise.

"No!" Sheldon howled, pulling him back down. "Let me. I'd rather die running than be left here alone."

Vince was amazed. "Are you serious?"

"I can't take much more." Sheldon did sound rather hysterical. "The thought of you dead and me lying here alone, with the shooting and the smoke . . . I can't take it!" He rose to a crouch.

"Shelley!"

"Please. I can't stay here."

"All right," Vince agreed reluctantly, proud of the dentist's unexpected courage. "But remember—serpentine!"

"Absolutely," Sheldon agreed and took off, zigzagging in the direction of the Senator's body. Alone on the open airfield, the dentist sensed even more gunfire and realized instinctively that without Vince he was the sole object of whatever weapons blasted down on him from the hill.

Up on the hillside, Carlos and Alfonso followed the tiny figure through their gunsights. They poured a steady stream of fortunately misdirected ammunition at him until they saw him reach the body of the late senator and sprawl beside it. Carlos smiled, preferring a stationary target, but Alfonso did not bother to react, his trigger finger continuing to pump away.

"You're dead, right?" Sheldon whispered to the corpse and, taking his lack of answer as agreement, whispered, "Okay." Trying to ignore what he was doing, he began to go through the dead man's pockets. On the second try he found the keys and started running back, thinking, My God! What if they're his house keys?

From behind the Mercedes, flat on his belly, Vince spurred him on. "Serpentine, baby, serpentine," he called above the gunfire.

On the hillside, seeing the figure getting away, Carlos cried, *"Carramba!"* and Alfonso cursed, *"Titopuente!"* but they gallantly kept firing.

"Got 'em," Sheldon half coughed as, doubled over like Quasimodo, he raced up to the car. He tossed the keys to Vince and they piled into the Mercedes. Keeping his head low, Vince inserted the key, started the engine. Just as the rear side window was blown out by gunfire, the car roared away.

"Desiste," Edgardo said, disgusted, up on the hillside. The two gunmen lowered their rifles.

"The general will be furious," Alfonso told his companions.

"There is still time," Edgardo snapped. *"Vamos."*

The three men jumped off and into the old black sedan and drove off.

The iguana heaved a sigh of relief, came out from behind the rock, and, forgetting breakfast, decided to move to a lair in a less built-up and commercial neighborhood.

Sheldon sat rigidly unmoving in the front passenger seat of the Mercedes, totally unable to absorb the sight of the rich tropical vegetation all around him as the car sped down the highway.

"I thought we'd go into town, check into a hotel, and relax," Vince said conversationally from behind the wheel.

Without changing his position, Sheldon fainted.

"Then I'll make a coupla phone calls," Vince continued, "and we'll wipe up the whole thing."

In 1935 the Savoy-Tegucigalpa had been the show-place of the city. Indeed, through fire, flood, revolution, and termites it had remained the best hotel, largely because no other had been constructed.

On the dangerously sagging terrace of one of the higher-priced rooms, Sheldon paced up and down. He ignored the magnificent spectacle of downtown Tegucigalpa, entirely uninterested in the busy street life of the palm-decorated, overheated metropolis. He was tired, irritated, and anxious, longing deep inside him for familiar things. He paused for a moment and stared at his watch. "Ten o'clock," he mumbled, though there was no one there to hear him, and continued rather sentimentally, "X rays and a cleaning for Mr. Pearlman."

The sound of Vince Ricardo's voice trickled out from inside the room. Naturally, Sheldon thought bitterly, we're thousands of miles from home, he's abducted his in-law, we have witnessed a murder, we have almost been killed, and he's on the telephone. He listened a moment, allowing the sound to form into words.

"You can imagine how I felt, General," he heard, "seeing him dead on the runway like that."

Sheldon, in the bright tropic sun on the terrace, sneered. "You can imagine how I felt," he said under his breath, imitating the glowing insincerity in his roommate's voice.

"I agree," Vince's voice wafted out, riding the damp air like a palm frond. "It must've been anarchists."

"Sure. They wanted to kill us, that seemed obvious enough," Sheldon commented to the traffic below.

"Hookers?" Sheldon heard Vince say. "No, that's very

kind of you, General, but we're really anxious to wrap this up and go home . . ."

Making a firm decision, Sheldon told himself, "I've got to get away from this guy," and walked into the room. At half the price, the accommodation would have been tacky, and its foreign charm was not enhanced by the chickens wandering around on the floor. Irritated by the promenading poultry, Sheldon kicked at one that stepped across his foot. "Get out of here," he yelled, and the chicken squawked its way across the room.

Vince waved at Sheldon to keep the noise down. "As quickly as possible, General," he told the phone. "No, we'll take a cab. . . . You're where?" he asked, grabbing a pad and pencil. "501 United Fruit Boulevard," he repeated as he wrote. "Via the General García Toll Bridge. Fine. A very fitting monument to you, sir."

Sheldon snorted to himself, half-listening to Vince, half-formulating a plan for survival.

"Yeah . . ." Vince was saying. "Now you have the money? . . . Right. Ten million in an attaché case and ten million wrapped in two small packages of five million each. Perfect."

Perfect, Sheldon thought, biting on a thumbnail, if I could believe it. If I could believe any of this. Except for the fact I can see I'm not in my office doing Mr. Pearlman's teeth, I wouldn't believe it. Can I believe my own eyes, he wondered, then pushed the question away as preposterous. Well, I've got to do something, he told himself. Having at least one idea of what to do, he started for the door.

Attracted by the movement, Vince looked over from

the phone, covered the mouthpiece with his hand, and asked, "Where are you going?"

"Just down to the lobby. I want to get a magazine."

"All right," the master criminal replied, "but stay close. We'll be leaving soon."

"The sooner the better," Sheldon said sharply and left the room. As he closed the door he could hear Vince saying, "No, the Treasury doesn't know what hit 'em." Annoyed, Sheldon slammed the door hard. The report sounded like gunfire and he almost hit the floor, realized his mistake, and ran down the corridor.

He emerged from the rickety elevator after a down trip that on a normal day would have terrified him but after recent experiences seemed almost pleasant. The busy lobby of the Savoy-Tegucigalpa bustled with activity, businessmen and chickens alike squawking and moving about under the old-fashioned airplane-propeller-type fans as though their errands were of earth-shattering importance. Spying a row of pay telephones, Sheldon made as much of a beeline to them as possible through the throng. Reaching an empty booth, he looked over his shoulder and scanned the lobby, for what he wasn't quite sure, then slid into the booth, found a coin in his pocket, which he inserted into the phone, and dialed "O," hoping and assuming that Operator began the same way in Spanish as it did at home. A voice pronouncing an unintelligible question told him he was right.

"Operator?" he asked and then followed with a prayerful *"Habla usted inglés?"* exhausting his Spanish. "Good," he said, relieved to hear the answer. "I need the American Embassy, please. It's urgent. I'm in terrible danger." He listened to a reply that was incomprehensible, hoped it

150

meant what he hoped it meant, said, "Thank you," in case it did, and hung on, suddenly wondering whether it had been altogether safe to tell the operator he was in danger.

Upstairs, at the moment Sheldon picked up the lobby phone, Vince was saying, "See you soon, General," and hanging up the room phone. Pleased with the way the conversation had gone, he picked up his suit jacket and smiled as he slipped it on.

Across the city in the Office of Intelligence Services in the American Embassy, the phone was ringing. The embassy was an old Spanish hacienda which the government had done its best to Americanize. This consisted largely of installing file cabinets and air conditioners. The files worked but the air conditioners overloaded the circuits and had blown out twenty minutes after they were installed. As the window in the Office of Intelligence Services had been sealed hermetically around the cooling device, the office was considerably hotter than the rest of Tegucigalpa. Barry Lutz, the Intelligence Attaché, was blond, vigorous, and, though he certainly wasn't old, he had served his country long enough to know that his own creature comforts were of prime importance. Consequently, he spent as much time as possible in the corridor outside his office hoping to catch a breeze from a passing secretary.

There was little activity in the hall this particular morning, so the sound of the phone caught his attention at once. Sighing and pulling his loosened tie a little further down, he walked back to his desk.

"Barry Lutz, Intelligence, can I help you?" he asked the instrument.

"Mr. Lutz, you don't know me very well—at all, really.

151

You don't know me at all—" a very nervous voice burst into his ear.

"Could we take that again?" Barry, confused, asked the caller.

Sheldon cleared his throat. "Listen," he said, "I may not be that coherent but I'm very sincere. I'm a dentist from New York. I practice in Manhattan and live in Teaneck. That's New Jersey." Sheldon wanted the facts crystal clear. He felt that would make him sound more legit.

In his office, Lutz was puzzled. "Who is this?" he asked.

"I'm an ordinary and patriotic American citizen. Now the thing is," Sheldon continued, "I'm in Honduras right now—"

"In Tegucigalpa?"

"In Tegucigalpa, that's right," the patriotic dentist agreed with his unseen savior, "with someone who works for the CIA, and we practically got killed when we arrived." His voice was going up and he knew he was speaking too quickly to get the message across, but he could not contain himself. "And now we're about to see some general, and I'm pretty sure it's dangerous."

"Well, why are you with this person?" Lutz asked, trying to do his job but relatively sure he had some nut on the phone.

"What?" Sheldon asked. "I'm with him because . . ." Oh, God, he thought, it sounds so stupid. "Well, his son is about to marry my daughter, actually."

"Who is this person you're with?" Lutz asked reasonably.

"His name is Vince Ricardo and I was—why are you laughing?" Sheldon screamed in the hotel-lobby phone booth.

Above in the room, Vince picked up the little black bag and went out, closing the door behind him.

"You're with Vince Ricardo?" The Intelligence Attaché had managed to bring his hilarity down to a polite chuckle and could talk again. "How much insurance do you carry?"

So upset that he sounded like a 33⅓ record playing at 78, Sheldon squeaked, "What do you mean, insurance? Isn't Ricardo with the CIA?"

"Oh, Jesus, no. Not anymore," the voice of doom on the phone announced. "He was thrown out of the Agency late last year on a mental . . . A mental," he repeated, answering the screech that sounded like a question. "You heard me right."

Sheldon managed to ask, "Why?"

"He's a wild man, that's why," Lutz said. "He'd go into very dangerous situations without rhyme or reason and just improvise, you know?"

Silently, Sheldon nodded to the phone. He knew, he knew.

"Totally ass-backwards," the man was going on. "The worst thing was, we lost half a dozen agents who were teamed with him; horrible, gruesome deaths. So we finally let him go. You're with him right now?" The Intelligence man sounded as though he found it difficult to believe. "In Tegucigalpa? Is that right?"

If the worst comes to the worst and I faint again, Sheldon thought, at least I'll be sitting up. There isn't enough room to fall in this phone booth. He put a hand on the door for additional support, took a deep breath, and tried to sound rational so the guy would help him. "Yes, he's got some engravings," he said. "He's trying to crack some international currency thing. See," Sheldon tried to explain, "we're together by marriage; this isn't the kind of thing—" and, waiting for the man Lutz to finish a question, he continued, "No. I always thought he was a little strange, but he's also . . ." Sheldon searched for a word and came up with "lovable," which wasn't quite what he meant, but he figured it would have to do. "I mean," he began again.

"Sure he's lovable," Lutz cut across Sheldon, "but he's completely out of his mind. I could tell you stories . . ."

"Don't," Sheldon breathed weakly into the receiver.

"Listen, do yourself, do me, do your family a favor," the representative of his government told him. "Stay the hell away from him . . . Right," Lutz said and pulled his handkerchief out of his pocket and mopped his forehead. When the man on the wire finished his sentence, Lutz said, "Sure," heartily, added, "Glad to be of service," hung up, and laughed. "Poor bastard," he said aloud as he headed back out into the corridor.

Sheldon hung up wondering whether he was more scared than angry or vice versa. What the hell do I pay taxes for? he asked himself. He pulled the door of the phone booth open, stood up, and came out. In the oppressively hot lobby, he froze in his tracks. Vince was standing outside the booth in front of him, holding the little black bag, looking angry.

11

The four men stood in the Visitors' Parking Lot at McGraw Airfield outside Lodi, New Jersey, staring at the coral-colored car with the flame decals.

The parking meter said *Violation*.

The cop said, "I noticed the license number was on my APB sheet."

"He got away," T-man Thornton said, wondering where he could find another job, and if he did, would the money he earned be worth anything considering what the dentist could do to the economy with the stolen plates.

"Car didn't look like that before," Turin said, tracing his finger along one of the flame decals.

"Fantastic job," Daly said, thinking of his old green Chevrolet. "I wonder where he got it done."

"What'll I do with it?" the cop asked.

"Haul it in," Thornton answered. "If nobody picks it up, you can always exhibit it in a freak show."

"I'll call the tow truck," the cop said and went back to his car.

"Where do you think he went?" Turin asked his boss.

Thornton shrugged. "I'll go check at airport operations but I won't get anything. You go back to the two houses and stake 'em out again." The two men groaned. "What else is there?" Thornton demanded. "Our only hope is the wife, the daughter tries to contact him. Or the kid in the other house. Maybe he ties in somewhere. If either of them goes out, tail 'em."

"But—" Turin began.

"Tail 'em!" Thornton said and stalked off toward the airport terminal.

There was only one cab waiting in the midmorning heat in front of the Savoy-Tegucigalpa. The driver, young and strong and spectacularly ugly, leaned against the fender, eyes half shut, dreaming of the woman he loved, reliving in memory his magnificent performance of the night before. Reaching the climax of his memory, he sighed, remembering the exploding glow of warmth she had given him. What a woman, he thought in Spanish. Tonight again, he determined, we will renew our love, if only I get enough tips today to pay the madame.

Idly, he noticed another car pull in behind his. But not a taxi, no threat. A black sedan. The driver killed the motor, got out and came over to him. *"Qué es la hora?"* the man asked him.

The cab driver lifted his arm, looked at his watch, and did not see Alfonso, who was the other driver, pull out the blackjack. The words, "Ten-fifteen," were in the cab driver's mouth but he never uttered them.

Expertly, Alfonso smashed him over the head and adroitly caught his falling body. He was certain no one saw him as he dragged the fallen cabby over to some nearby shrubbery, dumped him behind it, took his cap, put it on, and began to struggle the limp body out of its jacket.

"I thought you were getting a magazine," Vince said to Sheldon, who was framed in the phone-booth door.

"All they had was *Hustler* in Spanish," the dentist replied. *"El Hustlero,"* he invented, to make it sound better.

"You made a call." Suspicion colored Vince's voice, and a trace of disappointment at his almost-in-law's lack of faith in him undercoated his tone.

"That's right," Sheldon said, figuring it was silly to deny it.

"You called the Agency."

Oh, hell, Sheldon thought. If he's crazy, he's crazy. Let it all hang out. "Yeah," he said.

"What did they say?"

"They said you were thrown out of the Agency because you are A: dangerous and B: crazy." I don't care anymore, Sheldon thought. All I want is to get out of Honduras alive.

"They really said that?" Vince sounded more interested than annoyed.

157

"That's right," Sheldon said firmly. He was surprised when Vince began to roar with laughter. It was the last reaction he had expected. Still, Sheldon knew what his objective was and, figuring there had to be a taxi out front, he jumped around Vince and raced toward the door.

With remarkable agility for such a chunky man, Vince responded at once, taking off through the crowded lobby after Sheldon. Seizing a moment when he had a clear path, he jumped mightily and landed on the dentist's back, riding him to the flowered, fake-Oriental carpet like a rodeo star downing a steer.

"Get off me!" Sheldon screamed.

"You don't have a heart condition or anything, Shel?" Vince asked solicitously.

"No!"

"Then I'm staying on for a minute," the flying ex-CIA man said. "Listen to me."

I will not. I will not listen to him no matter what he does, Sheldon thought, and dragged his arms up to put his hands over his ears.

Vince leaned closer to him and spoke louder. "You're a total stranger. You call up the Agency. What do you think they're going to tell you?"

Despite his resolve, Sheldon answered, "I don't know. I don't care!"

"You could be a foreign agent. What do they know?" Vince pointed out. "So they tell you that I'm washed up, out of the business, nuts."

"Are you going to get off me or not?" Sheldon was beginning to feel conspicuous. Also, he was not sure that he was not lying in some chickenshit.

"Not yet," Vince said. "They did the one-hundred-percent correct thing, telling you I was nuts. Do you understand that? That it was simply a fabrication?"

"If I say yes, will you get off me?" Sheldon bargained.

"If it's a sincere yes."

Sheldon took a deep breath and as sincerely as possible said, "I believe it, Vince. I believe it was simply a fabrication to throw me off the trail."

"I knew you'd understand," Vince said and got up. Sheldon rose, rubbing at the chickenshit on his shirt.

"Let's go," Vince said.

"No way."

Vince was startled. "What's that, 'no way'?"

Sheldon planted his feet firmly on the worn and dirty lobby carpet. "No way is no way. I'm off the case here. I'm finished with this nonsense."

"I just told you—" Vince began.

"What difference does it make? If you're in or out of the Agency; if you're sane or crazy; to me, it's irrelevant. I'm just not going any further with this."

"Shel, it's cut-and-dried now . . ."

"Sure," Sheldon said, making it clear that the word meant the opposite of what it said.

"It is," Vince protested. "We go to the general, lay these engravings on him . . ."

There's no arguing with the man, Sheldon thought. He simply won't listen. He only understands action. Action he wants, action I'll give him. Sheldon whirled and took off toward the door again, but with no more success than the first time. Almost immediately, the chunky man had overtaken him and wrestled him once more to the carpet. If he was in the CIA, Sheldon thought, they must give those guys some training.

"Shel," Vince said, making it mean, How could you do this to me?

"If it's so cut-and-dried, you don't need me, right?" Sheldon said from his awkward position, face mashed into the moldy fake-Oriental. "So go in peace. I'm catching a commercial flight home; if the Treasury Department is waiting for me, I'll tell them what little I know. They'll probably just feel sorry for me. But I will not be shot at any longer! Okay?"

Vince hung his head in obvious disappointment. "Okay. I can understand," he said, trying to be fair. "With your background and all . . ."

Feeling slightly ashamed, Sheldon said, "Listen, if you want, I'll wait in the hotel for you to come back; we'll fly home together. But no more shooting, no more chasing. From here on in, I'm an onlooker."

Sadly, Vince said, "Okay," and got up off Sheldon. They dusted themselves off, an awkward silence between them. Then suddenly, emotionally, Vince threw his arms around his in-law. "Just don't go home without me, huh, Shel?" he pleaded. "I couldn't take being rejected like that. We'll go back with Billy and Bing, have a few laughs?" His eyes looked almost teary. "Okay, Shel?"

Annoyed with himself but unable not to believe the man's sincerity, Sheldon nodded. "Okay," he said. "This'll be fast?"

"I should be back within the hour."

"All right," Sheldon said, a nagging voice inside him telling him it was still all wrong.

"That's terribly kind of you, Shel. I really appreciate it." Tearfully, Vince embraced Sheldon again, then turned and headed toward the street, carrying the black satchel.

Sheldon watched the chunky little man heading alone out to God knew what, and as Vince went through the door, he moved slowly to the front window of the lobby.

Vince saw the cab as soon as he emerged from the hotel into the blinding sunlight. The driver, leaning against the fender, looked up and caught Vince's eye. "Taxi, señor?" he called.

"*Sí*," Vince answered. "501 United Fruit Boulevard."

"*Muy bien*," Alfonso said and opened the door for the man with the black bag. As the passenger got in, Alfonso nodded slightly in the direction of Carlos and Edgardo standing near the black sedan behind the cab.

From the lobby window, Sheldon watched Vince enter the cab, noticed the driver's slight nod and followed his glance to the two men. He saw them move casually but too immediately to get into their car. They were smiling broadly, and as they opened the car door, Sheldon saw plainly that there were several rifles in the front seat.

"Oh, God!" Sheldon cried, understanding it all at once. Slowly the cab pulled away from the curb, the black sedan following it. "I can't—" Sheldon told himself and realized that even if he couldn't get involved, there were other things he couldn't let happen. He dashed madly through the lobby and the door. Coming out of the hotel, he sprinted wildly along the side of the building after the cab, which was already picking up speed.

"Vince! Stop!" he yelled, but the cab moved even faster. The phrase "These are the times that try men's souls" flashed through Sheldon's mind and, even as he thought he'd come up with the wrong quotation, he ran, picking up speed to make a jump he never thought he would or could have made.

There was a terrible THUNK inside the cab, making Vince think, "Earthquake," until he realized it came from above rather than below. "What the hell is that?" he asked, but his driver was mystified too.

Above them, Sheldon crawled painfully along the top of the cab toward the front. Behind him the two men in the black sedan were equally surprised.

"Es completamente loco," Edgardo announced. Carlos, driving, nodded in agreement. Edgardo, knowing any unexplainable event was easily explained as being detrimental to their purpose, leaned out of the window with his gun.

Alfonso, not able to understand the crash on the cab roof, drove on, singlemindedly, pulling the cab out into traffic. Above him, unseen by the cab's occupants, Sheldon crawled forward, managing to get a handhold on the metal arc that enclosed the taxi's sign. Now other drivers, accustomed to almost anything on the streets of Tegucigalpa, decided they were unused to men crawling on the roofs of moving cabs and began to honk their horns and point. Edgardo, unable to get a bead on Sheldon, pulled his gun inside the sedan muttering, *"Imposible,"* to Carlos.

With a strength that surprised him, Sheldon pulled himself forward on the metal arc, then managed to hitch his body over it and slide down, face first, over the windshield. Seeing Vince, he pounded on the glass for his attention. He already had it.

"Shelley!" Vince yelled, astounded at the sight of the dentist hanging upside down like a sloth from a moving vehicle.

Under the assumption that whoever was sliding around

on his windshield was not on his side, Alfonso reached for his gun. Seeing this, Vince grabbed the black bag and, leaning over into the front seat, smashed the driver over the head with it. Considering the weight of the engravings, Vince was not surprised that he had knocked the driver cold. Alfonso slid away from the steering wheel, allowing the cab to decide for itself where it wanted to go.

While he appreciated what Vince had just done for him, Sheldon was still upside down on a moving, driverless cab with nothing to cling to but a windshield wiper. As the cab plowed into and through a street market, he tried desperately to decide if he would be better off struggling back to the roof of the cab or sliding all the way down to the hood. The cab, taking the decision out of his hands, plowed into a fruit-and-vegetable wagon and came to a halt as Sheldon half-gainered with less than Olympic form onto a pile of oranges.

Vince was out of the cab almost before Sheldon had landed. Please God, he prayed, let the oranges be rotten and soft so he don't get hurt, and dashed to his friend. Behind him, the black sedan screeched to a halt, noisy enough to penetrate the frightened and angry cries of shoppers and vendors alike.

Carlos and Alfonso leaped from their car and plunged into the excited maelstrom of the market, wielding their rifles.

"You okay?" Vince asked, grabbing the dazed Sheldon's hand and pulling him from the pulp, the peel, and the pits.

With a squish worthy of Orange Julius, Sheldon rose. "I think so," he answered, although he wasn't sure. He was about to feel for broken bones when he heard several shots. By now he had known Vince long enough to know immediately that they were the targets.

The two men ducked down behind the cab. "This you can't blame on me," Vince told him. "You volunteered." Then, seemingly overcome by emotion, he cried, "And a wonderful gesture it was!" and hugged Sheldon, who was still too numb to respond. Dropping his arms from the dentist, Vince yelled, "Let's go," and opened the cab door. He hauled out the unconscious Alfonso and grabbed his rifle. He stood then, using the cab as cover, and fired back at the black sedan.

Carlos and Edgardo ducked down as shoppers, salesmen, pickpockets, and prostitutes fled screaming, not waiting to see if this was a revolution or a personal matter.

"In!" Vince yelled, and as Sheldon slipped into the passenger side of the cab, Vince circled toward the driver's side, keeping up a steady volley of bullets.

As Vince ceased fire long enough to get into the cab, Carlos and Edgardo rose, let off another burst of ammunition for good luck, and leaped back into their car.

Behind the wheel, Vince paused long enough to say with sincere admiration, "Shelley, what you did was magnificent."

"It was instinct," Sheldon told him, then, his mind clearing, his ability to size up the situation pragmatically returning, he focused in on what he had done. "I was crazy," he said.

Vince turned the ignition key, and the motor moaned and rattled but turned over at last. "It was pure heroism," he said in ringing tones. "Don't think that I don't know how deeply you feel about me." Sheldon, embarrassed, looked up to God for consolation. "It gives me such a warm feeling, Shel," Vince said, then checked the rear-view mirror. "Okay, hang on, this is gonna be a little rough."

Having given fair warning, Vince jammed the accelerator to the floor. The car plunged into the traffic over the scattered oranges, mashing and squeezing them, creating enough juice to drown Anita Bryant. As Vince weaved in and out of cars and cabs and carts, he could see in the rear-view mirror that the black sedan was keeping pace with him. Sheldon howled wordlessly at something in their path and put his hands over his eyes. Tearing his eyes from the rear-view mirror, Vince saw a large pig in front of them but humanely swerved the cab around the animal, righted it, and drove on.

"Don't they squeal when they die?" Sheldon asked.

"The pig is alive, Shel," Vince reassured him. "You know, I'm such a great driver, it's incomprehensible that they took my license away."

The pig, a relatively sensitive animal, stood stock-still in the center of the traffic, trying to recover from the shock of almost having turned to pork roast. Stuck behind it, Carlos in the black sedan pounded on the steering wheel in utter frustration, yelling, *"Pronto! Pronto!"*

Screw you, the pig thought and, with a certain dignity as befits the infirm, moved slowly out of the path of the car. Carlos pulled his foot off the brake and the sedan sped on.

Sheldon thought he saw a sign that read *"Norte a ——"* (somewhere with a Spanish name) as the cab catapulted up a highway entrance ramp. Head and foot down, Vince pushed the cab out into the flowing traffic, not even waiting for an opening, driving as though the passing cars could sense how desperate he was. Seconds later as they sped along, Vince checked the mirror and saw the black sedan bolt from the ramp and into their lane.

"Okay," he said as though enough was enough.

"Okay what?" Sheldon asked in terror and despair.

Vince gripped the wheel and made a hard-left turn across two lanes of traffic. From the cars around them, the screech of rubber on asphalt and protesting brake linings was deafening as the cab lurched across the grass divider and turned left again into the southbound highway.

Sheldon, bouncing crazily in the seat, managed to turn and stare out of the back window. Wide-eyed with fright, he turned back to the implacable driver and howled, "What are you doing?"

Since Carlos had been a sinister six-year-old at the Barrio *escuela,* no one had dared to call him *"pollo."* And while privately he could admit to himself that what he was about to do scared him shitless, Carlos could not permit a stupid gringo vermin to defy him. Taking a deep breath and murmuring, *"Madre de Dios!"* he pulled the steering wheel hard left and duplicated the gringo's maneuver. Edgardo, who was less concerned with appearances, closed his eyes and prayed. When he reopened them, the two cars were racing downhill on the southbound highway.

Seeing the black sedan reappear in the mirror, Vince said, "Okay," again, this time sounding positively annoyed. He slammed on the brakes and the car stopped dead on the highway.

"Why are we stopping?" Sheldon asked, afraid to know, afraid not to ask. As he watched, Vince threw the car into reverse and started backing up. "What?" Sheldon cried.

166

As the cab barreled up the road in reverse, a huge tractor-trailer crested the hill and came steaming down toward them at about seventy. If the truck driver saw the cab, he simply did not believe it. Pulling at the wheel, Vince managed to weave the cab around the truck. Having finished the maneuver to his satisfaction, he looked to his left and saw Edgardo in the passenger seat of the black sedan flash by, an astounded look on his evil face.

Finding it hard to believe that the cab had passed him in reverse, Edgardo called to Carlos and pointed. Carlos stared back along the way he had just come and saw cars and trucks braking abruptly, screeching to a halt, their horns a symphonic medley of fury.

Aware and pleased that Sheldon's eyes were closed— why should he get upset?—Vince hung out of the window, steering in reverse, one hand on the wheel, the other waving cars away. "Out of the way, please. Emergency!" he yelled, ignoring the fact that no one spoke English. He was enjoying himself thoroughly. This kinda thing is invigorating, he thought to himself, keeps ya from getting old.

"Este loco," Carlos breathed, but, knowing as the matador knows that he must meet the bull, he slammed his foot on the brake and jammed the stick back to reverse. He moved his foot to the accelerator and the sedan belched backwards into the stream of traffic.

With the authority of a man who knew he knew his job, Vince braked the cab, shifted gears and accelerated, pulling the wheel hard left again. The car lunged back across the grass divider and, turning left again, hurled itself into the northbound traffic.

"Vince, for chrissakes!" the dentist cried.

"Relax! I've done this a million times," Vince said.

Carlos figured if he made it, if he won the contest, when he caught the cab, he would, like a true matador, cut off its fenders and its tail light and dedicate them to his general. Having so decided, he braked and repeated the gringo's U-turn.

Waiting for it, seeing it, Vince and his cab, a mirror-image of the sedan, made yet another U-turn to the south-bound lane, cutting off a bus by inches.

"Holy shit!" Sheldon screamed.

"That was a little close. I'll admit it. I cut it a little fine." Vince indicated he was not totally pleased with his own performance. He checked the enemy in the rear-view mirror and, reacting sharply, stopped the car.

"Not again," Sheldon breathed.

"I have to," Vince told him and, leaning out of the window, threw the car into reverse and began backing up the hill again.

Carlos, a picture of Latin fury, slammed his fist against the dashboard. He was on the wrong road, going in the wrong direction from the crazy *Americano*. *"Es imposible!"* he yelled and pulled the wheel hard, crashing across the grass divider to the southbound highway. Gaining the opposite road amid a squeal of brakes and angry shouts, he put the car into reverse.

"No en reverso," Edgardo pleaded. *"En seguida!"*

Carlos smiled and nodded agreement. *"Sí, sí, en seguida!"* he said and pulled the wheel to the right, starting north on the southbound highway in the direction the enemy had gone. Edgardo, seeing a blind curve coming, began reciting prayers he had not thought of since his first (and last) communion. As they neared the curve, the two Hondurans were amazed to see the cab come sailing

168

around it in their direction. Vince, now in forward gear, was honking loudly, smiling and waving gaily in their direction as a final insult.

Enraged beyond sanity, Carlos grabbed his gun and fired at the cab, ignoring the honking of other cars, ignoring the angry cries and threats, ignoring, until a second before it hit him, the mammoth trailer-truck that zoomed around the curve.

It was as though the trailer truck was the bat, the black sedan the ball, and the impact the masterful connection by that Great Slugger in the Sky. The car sailed end over end across the infield of the southbound lanes, the outfield of the northbound lanes, and right out of the park over and down an embankment beside the highway.

There was the sound of a shattering impact, the boom of an explosion, and flames shot up, signaling a home run.

12

Knowing there wasn't a chance that she would fall asleep, Carol Kornpett had not set the alarm. At six forty-five, still wide-eyed, she had resolved to lie still for another fifteen minutes, decide what to do, and get up at seven and do it. It came as a terrible shock when she woke at ten past eleven.

As soon as she came awake, she thought of Sheldon. Obviously, he had not called; certainly the phone would have awakened her. He had never once in their whole married life stayed out overnight. Who shall I call? she thought. Should I call the police? Should I call Vince Ricardo? Should I call off the wedding?

Obviously, the first one to call was Ricardo. If she got

no satisfaction from him, she would call the police. Then she could decide what to do about the wedding.

She got out of bed, found the address book in her purse, climbed back into bed, found the number, and lifted the receiver. As she put her finger on the dial, she heard a voice in her ear: "Can you ever forgive me?"

Tommy! Carol recognized him at once. Realizing Barbara must have phoned him on her extension, Carol moved to replace the receiver as Tommy continued, "I did the worst thing I ever did in my whole life last night!" Yes, Carol thought, and you did it to my husband. "No," she heard her daughter moan. Carol was certain it had something to do with the black bag and Sheldon. Hating herself for doing it, she placed her hand over the mouthpiece and listened. I've never eavesdropped on Barbara in my whole life, she thought, but that boy has endangered my man and I've got to know.

"It was despicable," the little sneak was saying. "You're my fiancée. You should be able to depend on me."

And instead, Carol thought, you and your father were railroading Shelley.

"I understood," Barbara said. "In a sense it was the right thing to do."

THE RIGHT THING! Carol's mind reeled. To have your father abducted? Could it be . . . it's impossible, but could it be that his own daughter—my own daughter—was in on it? Whatever it was?

"I didn't want to hurt you," the boy said.

But you forced yourself, Carol thought.

"No, you—" Barbara protested. "It must've been painful for you."

Painful? Carol thought. That miserable little bastard

172

doesn't know the meaning of the word pain. But wait till I get through with him!

"I shouldn't have thought," Tommy said, "I should have just put my arms around you and loved you . . . and loved you . . . and loved you . . . and loved you . . . and loved you . . ."

"I know . . . I know . . . I know . . . I know . . ." Barbara answered, falling into his rhythm.

Oh, my God! Carol realized she had jumped to the wrong conclusion and should not be listening. But if I put the phone down now, they'll hear the little click.

"I need you . . . I need you . . . I need you . . ." The insistent rhythm was getting to Tommy. He could feel himself rising, but with no occasion to rise to.

"Yes . . . yes . . . yes . . . yes . . ." Barbara panted into the phone, moist things happening inside her.

Carol blushed. Good Lord, she thought, they're doing it over the phone.

"Now," Barbara demanded.

"Now?"

"I can't wait. Right away, Tommy."

"In the daytime?" He sounded startled.

"I want your body," Barbara howled.

Jesus, Carol thought, and she put the phone down on the pillow. But she could still hear.

"I'll pick you up in twenty minutes," the boy said.

"No. That takes too long." Barbara sounded desperate. "Drive straight to The Bushes."

No, Carol thought. Where were you brought up? At least make him take you to a hotel! Upset, she rose and walked to her dressing table, but in the quiet room the telephone voice pursued her. "I'll meet you there in ten minutes," Barbara was saying.

"I'm leaving now," Carol heard the boy in the tinny, distant squeak of the phone receiver.

"Me too," Barbara said, and Carol heard the phone click down. She went back to the bed and replaced the receiver. Should I stop her? But then I'd have to admit that I was listening. And what's the difference? They're getting married tomorrow. She deserves whatever happiness she can get, the poor, maybe fatherless girl. But, good heavens, Carol's thought veered sharply, she didn't even think about her father. And what about his father? Oh God!

She sat quietly waiting till she heard the clatter of Barbara making what she thought was a quiet exit down the stairs. There was a short pause, and then she heard the door from the kitchen to the garage slam, heard the garage door open and the car motor start and a splash of gravel as it shot out into the driveway.

Well, if she's gone, she's gone, Carol decided and dialed Jean Ricardo.

"Hello?" Jean Ricardo said.

"Hi. It's just me," Carol said brightly, not yet sure of how to get the information she needed. "Just wanted to say 'Hello.' "

"That's nice," Jean said. "Everything okay?"

"Fine," Carol said too hastily. "How's the groom?"

"Oh, he just ran out somewhere," Jean sighed. "I hope he isn't catching something. He looked flushed," she said, mother-worried.

The son of a bitch is in heat, Carol thought. "Listen,"

she said, deciding a direct approach was the best, "is Vince there?"

"No."

"I just wanted to ask him something," Carol vamped. "Expect him back soon?"

"I don't think so," Jean answered. "I think he's gone for the day. Can I help?"

"No," Carol's voice sank about an octave. "Nothing important," she said, trying to retrieve the brightness, and failing miserably.

"How's Sheldon?" Jean asked.

What does she mean by that, Carol wondered. "He's just fine," she answered and crossed her fingers. "Well, I have a million things . . . I just wanted to see how your side was holding up."

"Oh, business as usual . . ." Jean said.

Jesus Christ, is it that bad? Carol thought. She said, "Well, I'll see you tomorrow."

"Yes. Thanks for calling," Jean said and hung up, wondering what the hell that was about.

Carol put on her robe and went downstairs, thinking, Look, if they're together and Vince is dead, Jean would have mentioned it. And if Vince is alive, let's assume Shelley is. And if they're not together but Shelley has something of Vince's in the black bag, Vince will find him. She went into the kitchen. The clock said eleven-thirty, and she decided to wait an hour before doing anything else. By then, the mail will be here, she thought. Maybe Sheldon wrote.

There was a note on the kitchen table from Barbara. "Have gone to look for shoes," she had written, then crossed out the word "shoes" and replaced it with the word "Daddy."

"All brides are liars," Carol told the coffee pot.

Had Barbara known where to look, at that moment she could have found her father getting out of a rather beat-up-looking taxi with her father-in-law-to-be, in front of an enormous, palm-treed tropical estate. The two men picked their way across a parking lot filled with military vehicles and crossed a wide expanse of lawn on which numerous peacocks strolled and preened like living bric-a-brac.

When they reached the impressive entrance of the main building, Vince knocked. After a moment's hesitation an eye peered through a peephole at them. Vince identified himself, and they were admitted to a mammoth, ornate hallway by an equally mammoth but tacky military aide. Sheldon was impressed as they followed the aide down the hallway. The mansion was decorated in early Mussolini with an adjustment for the tropic weather. It was quite unlike any place he had ever seen. Dropping back a pace or two, Sheldon whispered to his companion, "What's the story on this guy?"

"The general?" Vince asked and answered himself: "A very interesting gentleman. Two things, Shel, don't say anything about his scar—"

"What kind of scar?"

"You'll see it, but don't see it, get my drift?" Vince asked. Sheldon nodded. "The other thing," Vince continued, "be sure and compliment his art collection."

They had come to a huge, hand-carved door, and the aide raised his ham hand and knocked twice. The door opened and General García himself appeared. He was balding and bearded, a medal hung from a ribbon round the open collar of his shirt. His uniform was neatly pressed, braided and beribboned. He looked, Sheldon decided, like Castro just back from the dry cleaner. Above his beard on his right cheek, there was a large Z-shaped scar. Seeing Vince, the military man smiled broadly enough to accordion-pleat the Z and crowed, "My good friend!" as he embraced the chunky man.

Vince responded by crying, "General!" and Sheldon involuntarily said, "A 'Z'?"

The general wiped away the smile, allowing the Z its full space on his cheek. "What?" he demanded.

Vince made a hasty introduction. "General, I'd like you to meet Dr. Sheldon Kornpett, who has provided invaluable assistance on this mission."

The general eyed Sheldon suspiciously. Sheldon was unable to tear his eyes from the Z. He was trying to remember whether Zorro of "The Mark of . . ." fame was entirely fictitious or based on someone real. At last, the general bowed to the dentist, who nodded back hastily and smiled nervously.

"Dr. Kornpett." The general pronounced the name as though he did not intend to forget it. "Please, gentlemen, enter." He lifted his left hand in greeting. Vince and Sheldon could not help noticing there was a face drawn upon the forefinger and thumb. "You notice me friend?" the general asked.

Dammit, what was I supposed not to notice? Sheldon tried to remember.

The general made a fist, the eyes and mouth on his fingers came together, and the general introduced them as though they were a person. "This is Señor Pepe," he said.

Like that guy who used to be on the Sullivan show, Sheldon thought. "Eeesy for you, deefeecult for me." He remembered the entertainer's catchphrase but not his name. Seeing from the corner of his eye that Vince was studiously poker-faced, apparently playing along with the general, Sheldon followed suit.

The general looked into his fist and addressed it. "Shall we invite these men in?" he asked his fingers.

"*Sí, sí,*" he replied in a high-pitched voice, moving his thumb like a mouth.

"Do you like these men?" the general asked in normal, basso tones.

"Very much, very much," he boy-sopranoed back at himself.

He stole the guy's whole act, Sheldon thought. Or maybe he is that guy. I mean, where does that kind of act work when the Sullivan show goes off the air?

The general was smiling at him and Vince, letting them bask in the approval of his thumb and forefinger. He turned back to his hand and asked, "Would you like to give them a kiss?"

"Oh, *sí, sí,*" the thumb articulated. The general stepped forward and allowed his thumb and forefinger to brush Sheldon and Vince on the cheek as he made kissing sounds.

If this guy's in charge of this country, Sheldon thought, I can understand what they mean when they say Banana Republic.

"Is nice?" the general asked, and, conversing very rapidly in his two voices, answered, "Very nice."

"You like?"

"*Sí, sí.* They are very handsome."

The general put his fist down and laughed uproariously to indicate that the show was over. Sheldon smiled as much as he could in the circumstances, but Vince heroically managed to say, "General, you're extremely gifted." Sheldon felt a poke in his ribs from his companion and nodded in agreement.

The general looked as though Vince had just handed him an Emmy award. *"Gracias,"* he said. "We go in," as if the whole performance had been an oral examination the two Americanos had passed. He turned and entered his office.

Sheldon, pausing in the doorway, said, "Holy shit, he's crazy," under his breath.

"Don't underestimate him," Vince warned, and they followed the general into the room. It was large and stuffed with gilded and gaudy furniture that seemed to scream "cheap reproduction." However, the effect of the furniture was muted by the general's "art collection." Displayed on the white walls, in what seemed to be specially constructed niches, on easels, each with its own little electric light affixed to the top of its ornate frame, was an entire world of oils painted on black velvet.

The general allowed a pause during which they were to be awed by the room. The two men looked around, certifiably awestruck, and thought about what they could possibly say.

"General,"—Vince, as usual, was the first to come up with something usable—"your art collection always takes my breath away."

"Lovely," Sheldon breathed. "That toreador, it's very unusual."

Pleased, the general smiled broadly and walked to a huge swath of black velvet that had been desecrated with the image of a toreador and a fiercely charging bull. The general raised his hand to the painting as though he expected it to bow and proudly announced, "This cost me fifty thousand dollars."

"What a schmuck," Sheldon whispered, across the room.

"Shut up," Vince hissed back, hardly moving his lips.

The general moved along the hallowed wall and pointed to another treasure. "This tiger I recently purchased for only twenty-five thousand." He sounded as though he could still barely believe his luck. "I believe it is one of his best," he continued. "Note the plasticity, the almost Renaissance use of perspective."

"And he got the stripes perfectly," Sheldon nodded.

"That's right, Shel," Vince enthused, relieved his inexperienced companion was catching on. "And look at those whiskers; you could almost reach out and touch them," he said with wonder in his voice. Then his tone changed to that of a man who knew what was what. "That's the tipoff that it's a great piece of art."

"It's a masterpiece, General," Sheldon said firmly, understanding by now he could say any ridiculous thing as long as it was flattering.

The general looked very happy with his guests, his beard bristling in a joyous smile. "Not everybody appreciates great art."

"There's a lot of boors in the world," Sheldon admitted.

"You can say that twice," the general told him. "I

commission this man to do a new flag for our country, there is such screaming . . . I show you." Quickly he turned and walked to a curtain behind his desk. With the solemnity of one unveiling a newly discovered Rembrandt, he pulled a string and stepped aside so the Americanos could get the full effect.

The shock was almost too much for the two men, who were, after all, only a humble dentist and unfrocked CIA man.

"That's . . . magnifico," Vince managed to gasp, and, struggling to keep straight faces, the two men stared at the proud banner. It was, of course, black velvet, with a highly idealized portrait of the general himself standing beside a black-haired woman for whom the word "topless" seemed inadequate. The highly detailed breasts had a firm, imperious look and were almost the size of intercontinental ballistic missiles. The lovingly highlit nipples seem to stand at patriotic attention.

"Now this . . . is a flag!" the general trumpeted in martial tones.

"Is that Mrs. General on the flag?" Sheldon asked inanely, but the general didn't seem to mind.

"No. She is a girl from the village. A prostitute. If it wasn't for the Church," he said, a cloud of irritation crossing his now stern visage, "this flag would already be flying at the UN. They stand in the way," he said, in a tone that told them how incredible the Church's position was.

"The world is full of reactionaries, General," Vince said, "but it's men like yourself . . ."

Losing interest in his new flag, the general rolled up his fist again and said to it, "What? You are thirsty?"

"Sí, sí," the fist answered. *"Yo quiero agua. Agua fría."*

Vince looked at Sheldon. "That means Señor Pepe wants cold water," he translated helpfully.

The general took a glass of water from his desk and poured it into the mouth of his imaginary friend. Sheldon and Vince watched dumbfounded as the water trickled down the general's sleeve.

"General," Vince said, hoping to get past the parlor tricks.

"Down to business, eh?"

"That's right." Vince smiled. "You have the money?"

The general, without answering, pushed a buzzer on his desk. Two security guards entered the room immediately. One carried an attaché case, the other, two small packages. They looked a little old and out of condition for their line of work.

"These are the best security men in the world," the general bragged. "They used to work for J. C. Penney in Detroit."

"I believe I once purchased a comb there," Vince said.

The general snapped his fingers and the man with the attaché case opened it, displaying its contents to the two Americanos. Sheldon gasped. The case was crammed with thousand-dollar bills. I never saw so much money in one place in my life, he thought. Not even in Monopoly.

As coldly as though he were examining cucumbers in a vegetable store, Vince flicked his fingers through the money.

"Ten million *exactamente*," the general said.

"And the other ten?" Vince asked.

The general snapped his fingers and the other security

guard handed Vince the two small packages. "Small enough?" the general asked.

"They're fine. Perfect." Vince put one in his inside pocket. "Shel?" he called and tossed the other one to the dentist.

"What's this?" Sheldon asked, fielding the package.

"Five million bucks. Just hang on to it," Vince said casually.

Sheldon gulped. "Five million?" What pocket is safe enough, he wondered.

Vince turned and handed the black bag over to the general. "General," he began formally, "it gave me great pleasure . . ." and dwindled out as he watched the bearded man grab the bag greedily and open it. The general took out one of the engravings and held it up to the light, examining it closely.

"Beautiful," he whispered reverentially.

"Made by Uncle Sam with his own greedy little fingers." Sheldon wondered why Vince sounded like a used-car salesman.

"Fantástico!" the general breathed. He pressed another button on the desk. The painting of the tiger rose into the ceiling smoothly, soundlessly. Behind it, Sheldon and Vince could see an enormous, gleaming bank-vault door. Appreciating their impressed expressions, the general asked graciously, "Would you like to see?"

"Love to," Vince answered enthusiastically. "Shel, you too. This is extremely educational."

The general moved to the vault door and inserted a computerized card into a slot. Dials turned, lights glowed, and slowly the vault door swung open.

Keeping an eye on the general across the room, Sheldon

tapped Vince and whispered, "Do we arrest him now?"

"Relax. We're not arresting anybody," Vince whispered back.

"What?"

"Just go with the flow, go with the flow."

"What flow?" the dentist asked, the familiar feeling of not knowing where he was beginning to seethe again in his stomach.

The general was looking at them now from beside the open vault door. "Would you care to inspect?" he asked with a wave of his hand into the vault.

"Gee, thanks, General," Vince said, gratitude and awe smarming all over his voice. With a nod to his stunned companion, he started for the vault. Preferring Vince to being alone, Sheldon hurried after the chunky man.

Though he was not much of a museumgoer, Sheldon recognized the ambience of the interior of the general's vault. The staggering collection of currency and engravings were displayed like the most valuable pieces of modern art. But that's what they are, Sheldon realized. Large shelves were neatly labeled in bilingual placards— "Suiza—Switzerland"—and like labels for England, France, West Germany. The shelf labeled "Estados Unidos—United States," was empty. The general watched as his two security guards quickly and efficiently arranged the new engravings on the shelf. Sorta like a Tiffany window, Vince thought, and looked at the general. His expression was the pleased satisfaction of a man who saw the completion of his life's work; he was Isaac Newton rubbing his head after the apple fell on it; Alexander Graham Bell asking the operator for the first phone number; Reggie Jackson tearing the wrapper off the first candy bar.

"This is unbelievable," Vince announced. "General, I'm really impressed."

"*Finito,*" the general said, moving an engraving an eighth of an inch into alignment. "We are ready."

Fascinated in spite of himself, Sheldon asked, "How much are you going to run off?"

"Three hundred billion," the general said in round tones.

Vince nodded sagely. "That's more than enough."

"That's plenty," Sheldon agreed.

The general beamed, passing from awe at his own accomplishment to jubilance at a job well done. "Is a lot, huh?" he asked. "We will bring the Western banks to their knees." In an excess of enthusiasm, he threw his arms around Sheldon and Vince. "Me and my good friends from America," he said, sharing the credit generously.

"It's a wonderful thing, General," Vince told him.

"I didn't think I'd be this proud," Sheldon admitted.

"In seventy-two hours," the general intoned, "the monetary system of the world will collapse like a wet taco."

"A very fine analogy, sir . . ." Vince complimented him.

Becoming even more excited, the general allowed his imagination to run riot. "Blood will run in the streets of Zurich, German bankers will throw themselves under the trolley, widows and orphans will be left penniless . . ."

"Sounds good to me!" Sheldon felt obliged to say something.

"There will be panic and looting," the general continued, his voice rising, "rioting in the streets, suicides . . ."

"Fabulous!" Vince breathed.

"And you, my friends, you were here right at the start."

Sheldon nodded his head. "Something to tell our grandchildren," he said.

Unable to contain himself, the general hugged his good American friends. An expression of almost childlike delight and joy suffused the bearded face; the slashing scar on his cheek writhed and wriggled and, to Sheldon's eyes, seemed to change from a "Z" to a "$." Hugging the two men, the general cried excitedly, "We celebrate!"

Clasped in the general's warm embrace, the medallions digging into his chest, the overripe scent of the man beginning to get to him, Sheldon thought, I know he's an international crook but there is something sweet about him.

> *"I think that I shall never see*
> *A poem lovely as a tree . . ."*

The rich, full voices sang out, masculine and throbbing, although the second tenor was flat and the Honduran accents made something of a hash of the lyrics. A young lieutenant conducted the soldiers with great vigor and animation, extravagant gestures and a good deal of perspiration. Personally, the lieutenant preferred "La Cucaracha," and, for the occasional ballad, "Cielito Lindo," but if the general wanted foreign music then he would pull it out of the troops under his command. He made a mental note to tell the second tenor there would be no more weekend passes until he stayed on pitch.

186

Far enough away to make the music a gentle background to their conversation, the general entertained the two Americanos at lunch. Although they were seated in the confines on a small bullring on the estate, the heavy, round table was set as for an embassy party. The best of the general's china and crystal graced the linen cloth; their chairs were heavy, solid, intricately carved. There were flowers and candlesticks, the function of which was obviated by the bright sunshine. Behind them on a serving table rested the general's silver tea service, and on a brass tea cart was a large selection of his best liquor.

They deserve the best, the general thought, in the circumstances. Almost as though he had heard what the general was thinking, Ricardo looked at his watch again. The general turned to the other, the even stupider Americano, who seemed quite happy, even giddy. On what? The General wondered. The excitement of the moment? The chianti? Or just on his own stupidity? Enjoy, enjoy, the general thought, I will feel better if you enjoy this meal. The Second Battalion Glee Club continued their song. I suppose it's pleasant, the general thought, uncertain because he was tone-deaf.

"This is fantastic!" The Stupider One interrupted the general's train of thought. "How do you make this chicken?"

"Is old Tijadan recipe," his host replied. "Must be marinated for weeks."

"It's really exquisite," the guest said. "You can't get this kind of thing in New York." Without asking, Sheldon grabbed another piece of chicken and poured himself a little more wine. He noticed Vince looking at his watch again. Jeez, he thought, when you finally get a good meal and nobody's shooting at you, you turn into a party pooper.

"You are not hungry?" the general asked Vince. "You just pick." In an effort to lighten Ricardo's mood, the general lifted his balled fist and skidded up to his falsetto voice. "*Sí, sí*. He just picks." "He no like the food?" in baritone, and the soprano reply, "No. He no like the food."

The general and Sheldon laughed heartily, but Vince just smiled wanly, as though within his heart, he had a secret sorrow.

"Amazing how you do that," Sheldon said around a mouthful of chicken.

"The food is terrific," Vince said, "but my stomach's been a little upset." He gestured vaguely in its direction. "I'm supposed to stay away from all marinated poultry." Suddenly he cocked his head, listening intently and asked, "Did I just hear a doorbell?"

"But only God can make a treeeeeee!"

The general and Sheldon looked in the direction of the chorus and applauded enthusiastically. Vince just nodded. "They're extremely gifted," he said.

"Marvelous," Sheldon upped him one. "They're as good as the Mormon Tabernacle."

The lieutenant bowed in the distance, turned, lifted his hands and gave a downbeat.

> *"Buffalo gals woncha come out tonight,*
> *Woncha come out tonight?"*

sang the Glee Club of the Second Battalion of the Honduran Army.

188

"'Buffalo Gals'!" Sheldon was delighted. "We used to sing that in camp!" Swallowing some chicken, he hummed along, *"Come out tonight . . ."* as Vince looked at his watch again.

"General, what's the traffic like this time of day?" he asked.

"I danced with a gal with a hole in her stocking . . ." Sheldon sang, as he waved a chicken bone like a baton. The general rose.

"And now, my friends, a special surprise. Please follow me," he said and left the table.

Sheldon dropped his bone, finished the wine in his glass, and got up, eager to see what new treat the general had in store for them. Vince rose more slowly, reflectively, looking definitely worried.

"You know, this has been an amazing afternoon," Sheldon said. "This guy may be a big dictator but he really has a kind of innocence . . ."

Preoccupied, Vince answered, "Oh yes, he's extremely innocent," and cocked his head as if listening for something again. "I think my hearing's shot. Shel, did you just hear a helicopter?"

"No. Why?"

"Gentlemen . . ." the innocent dictator called, anxious to get on to the next event.

Sheldon looked over to his host, who was standing now beside an easel on which rested two gleaming medallions affixed to long ribbons. "Hey," he said, delighted, "he's going to give us a medal." Sheldon and Vince started over to the general. The Glee Club members were humming their way through another chorus of "Buffalo Gals," doing their best to sound like Muzak.

"You said something about a surprise . . ." Vince said as they came up to the general.

"My friends," the military man intoned and picked up the medallions. "I would like to present you with the coveted General García Medal of Freedom . . ."

Sheldon, squinting into the sun, took a closer look at the first medal he had won since the Good Conduct one Unce Sam gave him upon his discharge. It repeated the motif of the General's flag design: a picture of himself with his arm around a large-breasted hooker.

"Oh, General . . ." Vince said, sounding as impressed as he could manage.

But the dentist was truly excited. "This is an incredible honor," he gargled.

"To my wonderful American friends," the general rhapsodized as he hung the medaled ribbons around their necks.

"I danced with a gal with a hole in her stocking . . ." the choir trumpeted in honor of the Americans.

"My brave American friends," the general continued, "who will die here today as heroes." He nodded, and like magician's helpers two soldiers materialized behind his brave American friends and handcuffed them. Vince and Sheldon were stunned, though, Vince would have admitted, Sheldon looked more stunned than he did.

"Gentlemen, may I share something with you from my heart," their host-murderer began in a tone suitable for a funeral oration. "I am a pacifist by nature, with a deep Quaker belief in the sanctity of human life. I wish," he said, his voice trembling with emotion, "I had a choice but to kill you. *Vaya con Dios*," he concluded, on a religious note, and kissed the two men on both cheeks.

190

"Excuse me?" Sheldon said with his last shred of hope.

Vince took the hope away with a curt comment. "You heard right."

"And her heel kep' rockin' to the moooooon," the Second Battalion Glee Club concluded.

The lieutenant put down his baton and, without bothering to milk the audience for applause, executed a smart left turn, marched to the side of his men, left-faced, and stood rigidly at attention facing Sheldon and Vince.

"Firing squad, hey-utt!" he ordered.

13

Daytime manager of The Bushes was the best job
Verna Savage ever had. The night manager got the drunks,
the pot parties, the orgies, and the police raids. Verna's
ten-to-six shift was a breeze except that, since there was
no maid, she had to change the sheets a lot. It was a far
cry from her years in the chorus of the *Ice Capades*. I was
a schmuck, Verna often thought, to drag my ass around
the ice twice a day, when I coulda sat here, watchin' the
soaps and eatin' Mars Bars for a hundred and a half a week
and tips. Days, the only interruptions to *Ryan's Hope* and
The Edge of Night were occasional cheating housewives
out for a quickie and, from three to six, the high-school
kids, who tipped if she pretended to be memorizing their
license numbers.

Saturdays, when the TV was heavy on cartoons and boring, the work was absolutely zilch. The regular Bushes clientele, Verna figured, were resting up for a really big Saturday night. So Verna was surprised this Saturday morning when two cars, one behind the other, suddenly zoomed into the central parking area. She watched idly from the window as this kid, maybe twenty-two, good-looking but disheveled, leaped out of a Volks. He pulled up his slacks and pushed his shirttails in and ran toward the Toyota that had followed him in. Verna noticed his sneakers were untied, the laces flapping as he ran.

The manager could still hear the motor of the Toyota turning over as a young, pretty girl got out of it. She embraced the boy eagerly, her hands on his back working the shirttails out of his slacks again. The girl herself was dressed in jeans and a T-shirt. She was barefoot, Verna noted. These kids, Verna thought, scratching the dark roots of her golden hair, they don't know how to dress. I mean, where's the romance? She smoothed out her house-dress and slipped her feet into the green plastic thongs as she saw the girl point to the office and the boy start in her direction. The girl hung back in the shade of one of the cabins. Verna rose and went to the desk.

The boy tumbled in the door, asking, "You got a room?"

"Fa you, honey, anytime," she answered and wheeled the registration pad around to face him. "How many days you plan to stay with us?" she asked. Sometimes it was fun to embarrass them, and the best thing on the TV was a rerun of *Huckleberry Hound*.

"Uhhhhh," the boy said, holding it for a long time as he collected his thoughts. Cute, Verna thought. "Just a couple hours," the boy said finally. "My wife and I need a nap. We're driving through."

"From where?" she asked, making it sound like polite chitchat.

"Maine!" he answered quickly. "To . . . to Acapulco."

"Long drive," Verna said sympathetically. "Why'd you take two cars?"

"We're returning one," he answered. "It's a rental." Before she could comment on the Jersey licenses, he asked, "Where do I sign?"

"Right there."

The boy scratched a name on the card and whirled it back to face Verna. "Mr. and Mrs. F. Lee Bailey," she read. "Law student, huh?" she asked the kid, who blushed. Verna considered a blush a win in her private game and got off his back. "That'll be fifteen bucks," she said and, handing him the key, took the money and said, "Cabin Five." The kid ran out of the office. "Make all the noise you want, we're empty," she called after him.

"Jesus," Tommy muttered, rushing across the small concrete bay surrounded on three sides by cabins. He stuffed his wallet back in his jeans pocket and called, "Five," to Barbara, who was standing by a cabin door marked *Two*. She walked along the front of the cabins, meeting him at the door to *Five*. Fumbling nervously at the keyhole, Tommy managed to unlock the door and opened it for the girl. She walked through the door, turning just inside to face Tommy. He closed the door and she threw herself into his arms, kissing him, openmouthed, until he trembled even more violently.

"The blinds," he said, pulling his mouth away from hers, and turning away, he locked the door. Then he ran to the window and pulled the cord of the tin venetian blind free and let it clatter down. He reached across the window, pulling the opposite string, making the slats face up, dimming the room to a sort of dusty dark. He turned back to the bed. Barbara was standing at the foot of the double bed. She had already removed her T-shirt. Her beautiful, firm, high-standing breasts quivered at him, the nipples seeming to wink in the semi-dark of the room.

"My God, you're beautiful," he breathed and ran to her, taking her in his arms, holding her against him, feeling the smooth, soft skin of her back, kissing her for a long time. At last, she took her mouth from his and moved her head to his shoulder, whispering into his ear, "I love you so much."

"I love you," he whispered back, running his fingers down her spine, scratching the silken skin lightly.

She leaned back again, bringing her hands around his body to the top button of his sports shirt. She had unbuttoned two of them when he said, "Take it slow. Let's make it last a long time."

Turin drove slowly up to the entrance of the motel. He had followed the Toyota at some distance, not wanting to lose the car, not wanting to arouse suspicion. He poked the car a little further until the center of the court came into view. Seeing the little car inside, Turin accelerated, drove another fifty yards or so, and parked. As he walked back to the motel entrance, he saw Daly's old green car across the road moving slowly, saw Daly looking into the motel parking area as he had done. He waved and Daly waved back, his thumb and forefinger making a circle, the other three fingers straight out, signaling that they were right, this was it.

He waited till Daly parked across the road and came over to him. "I guess we got 'em," he said.

"Well, they're sure makin' some connection," Daly agreed.

"Ya think they got the plates with 'em?" Turin asked.

"I dunno. They don't look like they'd be the ones printing 'em."

Turin nodded. "They don't look like they coulda snatched 'em, either. Maybe they're just, like . . . couriers. Y'know . . . deliverin'."

"Think we should wait 'n' see if somebody comes to pick 'em up?" Daly asked.

"Nah. I think we should grab 'em while they don't suspect. Jesus, if they got the plates with 'em and we blow it, Thornton'll have our ass."

"Maybe we should phone the office and ask him what to do," Daly suggested.

Turin shook his head. "Look, we call in, we say the two of them are locked in a motel, we got nothin'. We go get 'em, we get lucky and find the plates, we're heroes."

"What if we don't find the plates?"

"Then we call in," Turin said. "Let's go." He turned toward the motel office. Daly followed him in. An old broad in a housedress was sitting in a chair watching *Huckleberry Hound* on the TV. She looked up.

"I didn't hear your car," Verna said. The two guys, appearing like that, made her a little nervous. Almost all the guests were couples of opposite sexes. These two guys didn't look like they were interested in each other and there was always the chance of a daytime robbery. She stood up.

"Two kids just check in here?" Turin asked.

"No," she said immediately, deciding they were the

fathers. Verna had a romantic turn of mind and didn't like ratting on kids.

"One in a Toyota, the other's in a Volks," the man said.

"This ain't a garage, it's a motor hotel," Verna said rather grandly. Wearily, the man pulled out his wallet, flashed a card at her. "Cops?" she asked.

"Treasury Department," Turin said. "They here?"

"Cabin Five," Verna backtracked. Romance was one thing, the Feds were another. The two men turned to the door and she yelled, "Take the maid's key!" and threw it to the silent one. She didn't need any busting down of doors on her shift.

"Ya think we should knock?" Daly asked as they walked across the parking area.

"Surprise," Turin told him. "We got the key, we got the element of surprise. We may catch 'em red-handed."

"Now," Tommy murmured, standing in the same spot in front of the bed. They had undressed each other slowly. They had moved as if under water, making it last, because there weren't that many clothes to take off. Slowly they allowed the sensations of touch to rise from their fingertips to their brains and spread through their minds and bodies, building the anticipation of love.

"Yes," Barbara whispered back and kissed him. Then she turned from him and walked to the head of the bed. She lifted one corner of the spread and nodded to the boy. He walked to his side of the bed, facing her, and took that corner of the spread in his hand. Their eyes were glued to each other.

"Together," Barbara said, her voice tremulous with love and desire. She nodded once more and they both

198

pulled at the stained chenille bedspread. At the same moment, Barbara saw the door burst open behind Tommy, and suddenly there were two men in the room.

"Nobody move!" one of them called.

Barbara screamed and more or less covered herself with her half of the bedspread.

"Goddammit!" Tommy yelled and, turning, saw the strangers. Automatically, without thinking, he pulled the spread in his hand away from Barbara and held it in front of himself. Barbara yelled, "Hey!"

"Nice to see you again, Miss Kornpett," Turin said appreciatively.

"Tommy!" she yelled.

"Oh my God," he said and threw the spread back to her, folding his hands in front of himself as he turned back to the two intruders. "Get the hell out of here!" he yelled.

"We'll only be a minute, Miss Kornpett," Turin said.

Enraged, Tommy turned to his fiancée. "You know him?" he howled.

Barbara knew the man looked familiar but was unable to place him. She shrugged at Tommy, confused.

"Turin, Treasury Department," he reminded her.

"Oh, yes," she said politely, "how are you?"

"What the hell are you doing here?" Tommy screamed.

"Just havin' a little look around, Buster. Don't get excited," Daly said.

"I am excited."

"Yeah. I noticed," Daly told him. Tommy blushed.

Meanwhile, Turin was looking through the empty drawers of the one dresser in the room. "You got the stuff with you, Miss Kornpett?"

"What stuff? There isn't any stuff!" Tommy yelled. "Are you trying to pin a narcotics rap on us?"

"I don't have anything with me," Barbara said with as much dignity as the soiled chenille spread afforded her.

"I thought you said you were from the Treasury Department," Tommy continued.

"We are."

"Well, what the hell does the Treasury Department want with her?" Tommy demanded. "If she's behind in her income tax, this is a helluva way to run an audit."

"Somebody meeting you here, Miss Kornpett?" Turin asked imperturbably.

"No," she said grandly. "I'm here on personal business." Turin giggled. Tommy balled his fists and took a step in the man's direction.

Daly put a hand on his arm and looked at his partner. "Ya think we should frisk 'em?"

Turin looked at the stark-naked boy and said, "I don't think that's necessary."

Tommy dropped his hands and covered himself again. "What do you want?" he asked.

"The mint is missing some engravings," Turin told him. "We have reason to believe Miss Kornpett has some information. We would like to know why she met you here today."

"Because," Tommy said with icy formality, "we had some things to discuss. Personal things. We're getting married tomorrow."

Daly looked at him. "I thought the groom wasn't supposed to see the bride before the ceremony," he said.

"I don't know anything about those damn engravings," Barbara said. "My mother found one in the cellar and she took it to the bank and that is all we know. Period. Now get the hell out of here."

"I'm sorry, Miss Kornpett. It just ain't that simple." Turin turned to Daly. "Keep an eye on them," he said.

"My pleasure. Where you going?"

"Gonna call in and see what's what," Turin told him and left the cabin. He walked back to the office where the blond was watching a rerun of *The Partridge Family*.

"Sorry to disturb ya," he said.

"It's fa kids," Verna said with a wave of her head at the TV set.

"Can I use your phone?"

"Help yourself." She nodded to the instrument.

Turin dialed and asked for Thornton. "I'm glad you called," Thornton began, when he came on the line.

"I followed the Kornpett kid to a motel," Turin reported, "where she rendezvoused with the kid from last night. The one in the Volks. I told you . . . ?"

"Yeah," Thornton sighed wearily. "We checked the license on that Volks. It belongs to Thomas J. Ricardo."

"Ricardo?" Turin repeated, the name sounding familiar.

"The son of Vince Ricardo," Thornton said and waited while Turin finished laughing. "So the Chief checked with the CIA and they're workin' on it. The kids don't mean a thing. You and Daly can come back in."

"Right," Turin said. "Jeez, I'm really sorry I busted in on 'em. If that boy is Ricardo's son, he deserves whatever he can get outa life." He hung up, nodded his thanks to the blond, and went back to the cabin.

"Okay, Daly," he said, opening the door and looking in. "Let's go."

"That's it?" Daly asked.

"Thornton says come on in. We won't bother you anymore. Sorry to have disturbed you, Miss Kornpett."

"Yeah," Daly said and turning at the door, added, "Go on with whatcha was doin'."

"I'll sue," Tommy told him. "As soon as I get out of law school, I'll sue the Treasury Department."

"Have a nice day," Daly answered and closed the door.

Tommy sat down abruptly on the foot of the bed. Barbara dropped her bedspread and moved to him, sitting beside him, taking his face in her hands and pulling it to her. "Like the man said," she said, "go on with what you were doing."

Tommy kissed her but after a moment broke the kiss, stood up, moved away toward the dresser. "I don't think I can," he said, ashamed. "I think the mood is broken."

"I know," she said despondently.

"I'm sorry. I'll be all right tomorrow."

"I know you will," she answered and pulled on her jeans. He was still standing in front of the dresser, idly flicking his finger at it. "Don't feel badly, Tommy," she said. "Obviously, God didn't want us to do it till after the wedding."

Carol, still sipping her coffee, had roamed into the living room hoping to see the mailman when he came. She was looking down the street for him when she was stunned to see the Toyota coming back. My God, she thought, that was even faster than last night. As she watched the car pull into the driveway, she thought, these kids . . . with all their permissiveness and sexy music and four-letter words in their movies, they don't know anything! Can't do anything! At least, can't do it right. Confirming

202

her worst suspicions, Barbara got out of the car looking hopelessly dejected. Carol put down the coffee mug and rushed to the front door.

As Barbara came in, her mother grabbed her, embraced her, and whispered tearily, "My poor baby."

"Something happened to Daddy!" Barbara said at once, frightened.

"No," Carol said.

"Then why did you say, 'My poor baby'?"

"Well . . ." Carol, knowing she was not supposed to know what she knew, vamped. "I was thinking about the wedding."

"Is there a wedding?" Barbara asked.

"Was it that bad?" Carol asked, and then could have bitten off her tongue.

"What?"

"Look, I've been thinking." Carol veered quickly in another direction. "Vince Ricardo is away."

"How do you know?"

"I called Jean. She said he was gone for the day but she was faking, I'm sure. He's away. Wherever."

"So?"

"So I think Daddy is with him."

"Caught in the jaws of a tsetse fly?" Barbara asked bitterly.

"Stop that. I know Vince is crazy and unreliable and that's why Daddy hasn't been able to call. But if anything were really wrong, we'd've read about it in the newspapers. I mean—" Carol faltered a little, felt herself on the verge of tears, took a deep breath, and went on. "If it's important enough for the Treasury Department to have come here, it would be important enough for Walter

Cronkite to have mentioned."

"Oh," Barbara said, remembering, "the Treasury Department has stopped tailing us."

"Tailing you?"

"They followed us last night. And Tommy when he left."

"Why didn't you tell me?"

"I didn't want to worry you."

"Thanks," Carol said, remembering her sleepless night.

"Well, anyway, they stopped," Barbara told her.

"How do you know?"

It occurred to Barbara that she couldn't tell her mother about the scene at The Bushes. "Can I have some coffee?" she asked and followed Carol to the kitchen.

"How do you know?" Carol asked, pouring.

"Well, when I left, they didn't follow me."

"And Tommy?"

"I spoke to him," Barbara said and took a long sip of coffee. "They aren't following him either."

"Well, then." Carol tried to look delighted that her daughter was lying to her. "Well, whatever it was is over. We will definitely go on with the wedding." Now is the time to tell me if you want to, she thought.

"What if Daddy doesn't get back in time?" was all Barbara said.

Well, if it makes her happy, it makes her happy, Carol decided, and she said, "Don't worry, baby, nothing short of a firing squad could keep Daddy away from your wedding."

14

As soon as the lieutenant had executed his march from center to stage right of the Second Battalion Glee Club and called out the order, "Firing squad, hey-utt!" a change came over his men that was almost as big as the alteration in Sheldon Kornpett's mood. As they came to attention, artists suddenly became assassins, musicians became murderers, and the flatting second tenor became Corporal Pablo "Dead-Eye" Lopez.

Sheldon was not surprised that he did not feel faint, since he simply could not believe what he was seeing. Again. He inched a little closer to his companion and from the side of his mouth asked, "What's our next move?"

"There's no more moves," Vince told him sadly. Then,

with an honesty that Sheldon regretted immediately, Vince admitted, "I made a big mistake."

With the beginning of belief, Sheldon felt the familiar Ricardo-induced rumbling in his stomach commence. "C'mon," he said sharply. "Stop bullshitting! Tell me something."

"This is it, Shel. That's all she wrote," Vince said philosophically.

"No fooling, Vince." The dentist's teeth were on edge. "What's the plan?"

Vince looked at him. "I'm wide open," he said. "What do you have in mind?"

The lieutenant's voice pulled their attention back to him. *"Presenten las armas!"* he cried into the sun that was not as warm as it had been before, though oddly Sheldon was sweating like a pig. He watched the soldiers bring their rifles up across their chests.

"Why don't we create some kind of diversion?" he suggested.

"Like what?"

"Why do you keep asking me?" Sheldon was having trouble keeping his voice down. "You're the big expert here."

Vince gave him a noblesse oblige shrug. "I'll give it a shot," he said.

"Ready!" the lieutenant cried across the field, and the choir lifted their rifles in unison.

"General . . ." Vince called, and when he was sure he had the man's attention, "may I interject here for a moment?" he asked.

"Yes?" García decided to listen. Grateful they had not yelled or screamed or struggled, he felt they deserved a little sniveling if that was what they wanted.

"General . . . spare this man," Vince cried, as impassioned as Barbara Frietchie, and pointed to Sheldon instead of a flag. Sheldon nodded as soon as the general looked at him. "Spare this man, Sheldon Kornpett," Vince continued. "Shelley, I call him," he larded in a moment's sentiment. "This man is a very great dentist from New York, a city in which, as you probably know, General, thousands of Spanish-speaking people stand in dire need of extensive bridgework. His death, I am afraid, would be a crushing blow to their hopes for a healthier set of teeth and gums." He nodded solemnly, emphasizing his point, and turned to Sheldon, mumbling under his breath, "That should do it."

The general sighed regretfully. "They will have great memories of him," he said, a little disappointed in Ricardo that he had not come up with a better pitch.

"That was it? The dentist thing?" Sheldon asked, and realizing that was, indeed, it, concluded, "I'm a dead man."

"I didn't promise," Vince began, and the lieutenant interrupted him by crying, "Aim!"

Sheldon stared into the barrels of enough rifles to outfit a men's choir and began to babble. "My whole life. This is it. Forty-three years old. I only had four women, two of them my wife; once before, once after . . . Even in the service . . . Her father, that son of a bitch, I never told him off. He's dead now . . . me, too."

Vince looked appealingly to the general, seeming by his manner to display Sheldon's turmoil and to plead for its relief. "General," he finally said, "I'm not one to pat myself on the back, but I could've told you he was going to blow higher than a kite. He's simply not equipped . . ."

Sheldon, involved as he was in his own problems, didn't hear Vince. Hardly realizing he was verbalizing his thoughts, he droned on. "My office, all the equipment. The magazine subscriptions, they're all for four, five years. They'll just keep coming . . ." Somehow he saw swarms of *National Geographic*s flying into an empty, dusty waiting room. "My BMW," he remembered. "It's a thirty-six-month lease . . . the Germans don't care if I'm dead . . ."

"General, don't you have a sedative for Shel?" Vince pleaded. "This isn't right."

Sheldon heard him. "No drugs," he said. "Not allowed."

"An aspirin, then." Vince was willing to settle for small comforts.

The general snapped his fingers and ordered, "Bandannas," but by then Sheldon remembered the paint job on the BMW and wondered what they'd do to Carol when she tried to return it when the lease was up.

Two soldiers, seeming almost to move to the sprightly rhythm of "Fine and Dandy," stepped forward, produced blindfolds, and tied them over the eyes of the hapless Americans.

"And we're supposed to have cigarettes," Vince reminded them. From out of nowhere the two soldiers popped cigarettes into the men's mouths.

"No thanks. I never smoke," Sheldon told them and spit his out.

The general nodded at the lieutenant, who ordered his men to "Aim!" again.

"I really hope there's a God," Sheldon said.

"Me too, Shel. And I hope He's got a sense of humor."

The general nodded toward the lieutenant for the last time.

"Fire!"

The thunderous explosion of gunfire rattled the lunch dishes, shook the palms, dislodged a myriad of birds, and set dogs at unseen distances to barking. The noise would have seemed far greater than the number of guns the Second Battalion Glee Club possessed, had their unfortunate targets been pragmatic enough to count decibels.

As it was, target Sheldon Kornpett screamed, "I'm hit!" and fell to the ground in the little bullring. Then, seeking to localize the pain, running a mental roster of his arms, legs, and trunk, he realized there was no pain. "Maybe I'm not hit," he said, confused.

"I'm definitely not hit," the cooler Vince Ricardo announced and dived for the dirt.

Blindfolded and handcuffed, the two men crawled around in the dirt, dragging their General García Medals of Freedom in the dust. They remained unaware that the warm, tropic scene of their demise had been invaded by a posse of jeeps, the word *Interpol* inscribed on their dusty sides. Interpol troops had leaped from the jeeps, their guns blazing at General García's soldiers even before they hit the ground.

"What the hell is happening?" Sheldon yelled.

"We got bailed out," Vince called back to his unseen in-law. "Stay down," he ordered. "Serpentine!"

Oh shit, that again, Sheldon thought, but did as he was told.

Obviously the Glee Club had spent too much time practicing their arpeggios, because their marksmanship was no match for the Interpol forces. Seeing that the General's troops were getting much the worst of it and seemed near collapse, the blond man in the command jeep drove to the end of the bullring. He stepped out of the

209

jeep, checked his watch, and looked around the enclosed area.

Behind him the lieutenant-conductor was waving a white hanky as his songbirds moulted their rifles. Others of the Interpol troops detached themselves from the main party and ran to the general, who was too dismayed to do anything but allow himself to be handcuffed.

The blond man saw the two Americans, still cuffed and blindfolded, writhing in the dust of the bullring and ran up to them calling, "Vince?"

"Barry?"

"You can get up," Barry said. "It's all over."

"Shel, we can get up," Vince repeated. The two men staggered awkwardly to their feet and Barry removed their blindfolds and their handcuffs. Vince's uncovered eyes were blazing. "Where the hell were you?" he demanded. "We almost got croaked here!"

"The traffic was unbelievable," Barry apologized.

Sheldon, too, found some reason to be annoyed. With Vince. "You knew they were coming?"

"You're Sheldon Kornpett?" the blond man asked.

"That's right," Sheldon said, still sure of that, at least.

"Barry Lutz," the other man said, extending his hand.

"The guy I spoke to on the phone?"

"Sorry to give you the runaround," Lutz said, "but I'm sure you understand now. Vince, where are the engravings?"

"He's got a vault behind a tiger painting," Vince told him. "You know we almost got killed here?" He still couldn't seem to get over that.

Sheldon, who was finding it hard to think straight, asked, "That was all a story about Vince?"

"We really had to keep you in the dark, Sheldon," the blond man said and turned to Ricardo. "Vince, where's the money?"

Vince wiped the dust from his eyes and looked around the bullring. At last he saw the attaché case in the dirt, picked it up, and handed it to Lutz. "Here were are. The whole schmear."

Sheldon began, "And we've got another—"

Rudely, Vince continued over his voice. "It's in thousands, in stacks of fifties."

"And there's more—" Sheldon began again, only to be further interrupted.

"Yeah, there's more to this story than I can tell you now, Bar," Vince said with a definite that-ends-the-conversation tone.

As the blond man opened the attaché case, Sheldon opened his mouth then suddenly shut it. Firmly. His eyes flicked back and forth as desperately he tried to organize his thoughts, understand the action.

"Beautiful," Lutz said, staring at the contents of the attaché case.

General García, both crestfallen and angry, was marched by, wearing his handcuffs with an ill grace. "There is another ten million," he called. "I give him twenty. Not ten, twenty."

"Of course, you did, General," Vince smiled, and tapped his temple, indicating to his friend Barry Lutz that the general was not playing with a full deck.

"Is true!" The general stood his ground. "This *bandido* has another ten!"

"C'mon, get that nut the hell out of here," Lutz ordered the Interpol agents.

"Is a crook," the general kept yelling, resentfully, as they pulled him off.

Suddenly Sheldon smiled, a big, beautiful, happy smile. He understood. The pot was calling the kettle black and he, Sheldon Kornpett, D.D.S., was half the kettle. And two minutes ago I was facing a firing squad, he remembered. Then, with a lack of originality excusable in the circumstances, he thought, Life's a funny business after all.

Lutz snapped the attaché case shut and looked at the two begrimed men in front of him. "Guys, you did fantastic work."

Sheldon was unable to control the incipient giggle, and unable to rein it in as it moved to loud guffaws. Vince seemed to understand. "Relieved, huh?" he asked.

"Tremendously," the dentist said as the guffaws blended on up into uncontrollable laughter.

"Great feeling, isn't it?" Lutz said warmly, understanding that the man, a civilian, had just been snatched from the jaws of death.

The uncontrollable laughter switched gears smoothly and went into the overdrive of hysteria. Vince, becoming a little uncomfortable as Sheldon's hilarity threatened to overwhelm them both, checked his watch.

"Listen," he said, "we'd love to hang around and shmooze, Bar, but it's a big day for us tomorrow. Our kids are getting married."

"So I've heard," Lutz replied.

"What a day!" Sheldon said, but wasn't sure whether it was today or tomorrow he referred to.

"Well, I couldn't be happier for both of you . . ." Lutz said and hesitated just a moment as if waiting for something. "So I won't see you till Wednesday," he said to Vince.

"Wednesday?"

"Next Wednesday," Lutz reminded him. "We've got a date in Peru."

"Uh . . . I don't think so, Bar." Vince began to walk, and Sheldon, at last controlling his laughter, hurried to catch up with him. "Sorry to run . . . but we've got a plane to catch." By now the two men were indeed running.

"Hey, wait a minute," Lutz called and took off after them when they did not stop.

Puffing just a little, Sheldon and Vince rounded the corner of General García's mansion and headed for the parking lot. They were halfway there when Lutz came into view again from behind the mansion.

"What do you mean?" he called. "You're quitting the Agency?"

Vince and Sheldon reached the cab. They turned and waited till Lutz got up to them. "I've had it, Bar," Vince said sincerely. "My kid's getting married, maybe there's gonna be grandchildren . . . I'm tired. It's over," he said, regretfully.

"Take a desk job," his colleague suggested.

Vince shook his head. "That's not for me. I'll tell you something else, I don't believe in this crap anymore. I mean, it used to be like cowboys and Indians, now . . . I almost died here today for the international money system. I mean, what the hell is that?"

"I agree," Sheldon backed up his in-law. "I think he should retire. For the family."

Lutz looked at Vince with some concern. "You can make it on your pension?"

"I'll give it a shot," Vince said and looked at Sheldon. They laughed with the freedom of kids, the maturity of men who'd made it, the total hysteria of a winning contestant on *The Price Is Right*.

Still laughing, they climbed into the cab and drove off, howling back down the highway.

Lutz watched the car until it disappeared, a puzzled expression on his face. I can't believe it, he thought. An old warhorse like Ricardo, retiring?

15

Workmen were setting up the chairs and the altar in the backyard, and Carol, with shaking fingers, was just starting to apply the second false eyelash. Her hair was in curlers but her makeup was on; she was wearing her bra and the half-slip her friend Bunny had been kind enough to get her yesterday at Sears. Evidently Bunny thought she was fatter than she was, but Carol had managed to pin it, painfully but unobtrusively. Halfway through the second eyelash, Barbara burst into her mother's room. "In all the excitement," she announced, "I forgot the shoes."

Cursing under her breath, Carol went to her closet and, on hands and knees, rooted among her own shoes for a pair of white pumps she was sure she hadn't thrown out and that would only be a size and a half too small. She found them finally under an Altman's box containing a dreadful Christmas present she was saving for her sister-in-law's anniversary. Turning to pitch them out to Barbara, she knocked off the half-on eyelash. "Try these," she called. Then the phone rang.

"I'll get it," Barbara said.

Crawling out of the closet backwards, Carol yelled, "I'll get it. You try the shoes." She rose and ran for the phone. "If it's your aunt Louise, I'll kill her. And find my eyelash in the closet." She grabbed the phone. "Hello," she snarled into the mouthpiece.

"It's me. I'm at the airport," she heard Shelley say.

"What airport?" she snapped. Then, realizing, she said, "Oh, Shelley! Thank God," and began to cry.

"Don't cry. You'll lose your eyelashes," he said.

"I did," she cried and looked at Barbara struggling into the shoes. "Find my eyelash," she called, and then, "It's Daddy."

"Where is he?"

"Where are you?" Carol repeated the question.

"I'm still at the airport."

"Oh, Shelley, I've been so worried—where were you?" she interrupted herself, the significance of an airport hitting her.

"I've only got one dime. I'll tell you later," her husband said. "Is everything set for the wedding?"

"Fine, just fine," Carol said automatically.

"Well, I just wanted you to know, I'll be there." Behind him Carol heard some whispered words and Shelley came back on the line to say, "Vince'll be there, too."

"You're with him?" Carol asked.

216

"Everything's fine. I'll tell you all about it when I get there. I love you," Shelley said and hung up.

"I love you, too," Carol said to the buzz and replaced the receiver. She turned to Barbara. "He's fine, he's at the airport, he's with Vince, they'll be here, where's my eyelash?" she said.

The guests were getting fidgety. They had all said, "Isn't it a perfect day for a wedding?" and "What would they have done if it rained?" and waited. They had walked around the garden and said, "How's Aunt Martha?" and "You remember Kevin? He was six years old and now he's got a moustache," and waited. They had seated themselves in the ranks of rented chairs and nodded to their neighbors and waited. Now they were saying, "What the hell's going on?" and "Goddamn hot in Teaneck," and "You think maybe he ditched her?"

Sheldon's brother-in-law, seated in the second row, looked at his watch and turned to his wife. "They're forty-five minutes late."

"You know Sheldon," Louise sighed, fanning herself with a Kleenex, "inconsiderate." She looked around the lawn at the perspiring wedding guests. "You'd think," she said, "if people are holding a wedding in their backyard, they'd at least put in air conditioning."

In the living room, Barbara, in a high-necked old-fashioned-looking wedding gown with net sleeves and a ribbon waistband and her mother's shoes that pinched, looked both gorgeous and very agitated. "We cannot wait anymore," she told her mother.

Carol looked lovely, too, though there was some dust on one of her eyelashes. She was as upset as the bride.

217

"What's with them?" she demanded. "They called from the airport two hours ago."

In the kitchen, the groom, who had removed his gray cutaway coat for the third time, looked handsome and nervous. "What did Vince pull this time?" he asked his mother.

Jean Ricardo blotted her lipstick. Her pearls rattled and the flower that grew out of the left shoulder of her dark dress shook. "Why do you assume it's your father's fault?" she snapped. Her son stared her down. She nodded. "Of course it's his fault."

She left the kitchen and walked through the entrance hall and down the steps into the living room just in time to hear Barbara say furiously, "I'll never forgive him."

Jean decided it was wiser not to ask who her daughter-in-law would never forgive. Instead she asked, "What do you think we should do?" Her ears were beginning to bother her, not exactly a ringing, more a droning.

Barbara came to a decision. "Let's get going. Maybe they'll make it for lunch."

"It's such a shame," Carol said, near tears.

But Jean could hardly hear her. The droning sound was getting worse. High blood pressure, Jean thought, and asked Carol, "What did you say?"

"I said it's a shame," Carol screamed, for now all three of the women could hear the droning.

Barbara rushed to the window, followed by the two mothers. Absolutely stunned, they saw a helicopter descending toward the front lawn. As they watched, the plane slowed its descent and hovered. Before their unbelieving eyes the three women saw Sheldon and Vince,

218

impeccably dressed in formal morning attire, being lowered from the helicopter.

"Jesus Christ," Carol mumbled.

The guests were standing now, gawking, muttering among themselves, the ladies holding their large hats to their heads against the wind from the rotors. They saw a Chinese pilot lean out of the cockpit of the aircraft.

Bing Wong yelled "Happy wedding" to Vince above the roar, although of course he yelled it in Chinese.

Vince yelled back the Chinese equivalent of "Thanks," the pilot saluted, and the craft rose and flew off. The two passengers started for the house, waving at the guests.

"Sorry we're late. Be right with you," Sheldon called in general apology.

"How were the hors d'oeuvres?" Vince asked the nearer guests as the two men raced for the house.

"Sheldon was always a show-off," his sister told her husband and sat down again to wait.

"Okay," Sheldon yelled, happily running into the living room.

Vince, behind him, said, "Thanks for waiting," and the two men embraced their wives.

"Shelley," Carol said, "two days—we were crazy—"

Sheldon stopped her. "Everything's terrific," he said and turned to his daughter. "You look so beautiful," he said as he hugged her.

Barbara began, "You're all—"

"I'm great," her father interrupted. "You don't know how great!"

"We have to start," Jean Ricardo reminded them.

Vince said, "Give the orchestra five minutes to set up."

"What orchestra?" Barbara asked.

"The New York Philharmonic," Sheldon said with a nothing-is-too-good-for-my-daughter smile.

"Shelley," Carol began, but then she heard the sound of tuning-up outside.

The guests watching the orchestra prepare itself were mumbling in absolute awe.

"And pretentious," Sheldon's sister continued her assessment of his character to her husband.

Drawn by the hubbub, Tommy was staring out of the kitchen window wondering who the crowd of musicians were and what it all meant. Hearing a sound behind him, he turned and saw his father. "Dad, where the hell have you been?"

Overcome by emotion, Vince hugged his boy, stepped back, and looked him over proudly. "You're really a man now," he said and reached over to straighten Tommy's tie. "Remember how we used to play ball on Nagle Avenue?"

"We never played ball on Nagle Avenue. We talked about playing ball on Nagle Avenue."

"Well, maybe this'll make up for it." Vince handed Tommy an envelope. A very bulky envelope. "From Shelley and me. Barbara got one too."

Outside the house, standing with her father, Barbara was staring down at the contents of an envelope exactly like the one in Tommy's hand. "Dad," she said, her voice shaking a little, "this is a million dollars."

"I know," he smiled, and nodded.

Vince came out of the house and joined them. He kissed his almost daughter-in-law and said, "I think I finally impressed my son."

"Dad," Barbara asked slowly, "is this all from root canals?"

Before Sheldon could think of a way not to answer, a long, official-looking black car pulled into the Kornpett's driveway and stopped in front of the three of them. A man stepped out of the car, confusing Barbara, who was sure she knew all the wedding guests and equally sure she had never seen this man before. The man surprised Vince, who, of course, knew Barry Lutz but had no idea why he was there. Sheldon, seeing the stern expression on Lutz's face, began to have some idea of why he was there, and this little inkling pushed the happy father to the very edge of nightmare from which he had so recently escaped.

Lutz stood before the three and spoke. "Vince, I'm just shocked and disappointed—"

"Barry, it's very simple—" Vince vamped.

"We counted wrong," Sheldon said, thinking, You could probably build a good defense on that.

Barbara looked at him, wondered why he was ashen. "Dad . . ."

"Barbara, maybe you should go inside."

"No," Lutz said, "I'd like your daughter to be here, Sheldon."

"Please . . ." Sheldon said and hoped he would not cry, at least not before the ceremony.

"Sheldon, I hardly know you, so I didn't know what to expect. But Vince . . ." Lutz turned to the one he knew better.

"Bar, will you listen to me?"

But Lutz plunged on. "After all the years we put in together, you pull something like this."

Sheldon decided to build the defense right now. "We were so nervous we couldn't count straight—"

"What is this about?" Barbara wanted to know.

"What is this about?" Lutz repeated her question

philosophically. Sheldon, not wanting to see Barbara's face, not wanting Lutz to see his, unable to look at Vince, moved his head in the only other direction it could go and stared down at his shoes. They were so highly polished he could see an almost perfect reflection of his own face, and he didn't like that either. "Your father-in-law and I," Lutz continued, while Sheldon arranged his head, "worked together for nearly twenty years, and what does he do after twenty years?"

"Barry . . ." Vince started to say.

"We were in such a hurry," Sheldon interrupted. "It looked like too little . . ."

"He doesn't invite me to his own son's wedding," Barry Lutz concluded.

Sheldon closed his eyes and there was a moment of stunned, grateful silence. When he was relatively sure he would not faint, he reopened his eyes and, checking in the reflection on his shoes, saw that the color had come back into his face. He looked up at Lutz and spoke. "It looked too little and it turned out to be one hundred and seven. I told Vince we had invited a hundred and twenty. My fault," he apologized.

Barbara looked at her father, an odd expression in her eyes. He nodded at her slightly and she turned to the strange man.

"We got screwed up. I remember Vince saying he wanted to invite you."

Sheldon was so proud of Barbara at that moment that he had to kiss her.

"You know how these things are, Bar"—Vince picked up the conversational thread—"with a family and all, aunts, uncles . . ."

222

For the first time since he had arrived, Lutz smiled. "Vince, can't you tell when I'm ribbing you?" He turned to Barbara. "Here," he said and handed her an envelope. "It's a little something from the boys at the Agency. A fifty-dollar savings bond."

"Oh, Barry . . ." Vince said, overcome.

"Thank you so much," Barbara echoed him.

"That's a wonderful gesture," her father threw in.

"I'm so touched, I . . ." Vince couldn't continue. For one thing, he saw Barbara take out the envelope containing the million and for another he saw Sheldon looking like he might faint again.

"I'll put it right in here for safekeeping," the bride said and slipped the bond in with the million.

When the New York Philharmonic plays "Here Comes the Bride," the familiar music somehow takes on an extra dimension. "They're too noisy," Sheldon's sister Louise said as she swiveled around with the other guests to see her niece in her wedding gown.

She was beautiful, but then, as Louise thought, for a girl not to be beautiful at her wedding, she'd have to be a real dog. Though her shoes were a size and a half too tight, Barbara smiled radiantly on the arm of her father, Sheldon Kornpett, D.D.S., millionaire. He was pretty radiant, too. As they came down the aisle in the peculiar lockstep saved for weddings and military funerals, they were followed by an equally beaming Vince, escorting a groom who was certain that he had love AND financial security.

Reaching the foot of the aisle of trampled grass, Sheldon, as though he had had time to rehearse, delivered

Barbara to the altar and stepped to one side. Vince deposited the groom beside the bride and moved to the opposite side facing Sheldon. The two happy fathers beamed at one another.

In the front row, Carol whispered to Jean Ricardo, "It's marvelous how close Shelley and Vince became."

The other mother nodded. "They have tremendous respect for each other."

The young couple turned to face each other, their hearts full of love, their imaginations racing ahead to the night at the Plaza, whose security would certainly keep their room free of T-men. Behind them, their fathers smiled at each other more and more broadly across the altar. The smiles were in distinct danger of turning into rip-roaring, undignified laughter, but if the two men actually did laugh, the New York Philharmonic drowned them out and nobody noticed.